4624

Alonso an

Macmillan Caribbean Writers

Alonso and the Drug Baron

EVAN JONES

MACMILLAN
CARIBBEAN

Macmillan Education
Between Towns Road, Oxford OX4 3PP
A division of Macmillan Publishers Limited
Companies and representatives throughout the world

www.macmillan-caribbean.com

ISBN-13 978-1-405031-75-2
ISBN-10 1-4050-3175-1

Text © Evan Jones 2006
Design and illustration © Macmillan Publishers Limited 2006

First published 2006

Typeset by EXPO Holdings
Cover design by Tim Gravestock and Karen Thorsen Hamer
Cover illustration by Tim Gravestock

Printed and bound in Thailand
2010 2009 2008 2007 2006
10 9 8 7 6 5 4 3 2 1

Series Preface

Evan Jones is perhaps best known throughout the Caribbean for his rousing *Song of the Banana Man*. Internationally he is known as the writer of many memorable feature films and plays for television. His new novel, *Alonso and the Drug Baron,* a Jamaican tale of drug smuggling and greed, murder and innocence, is fast-paced and very funny. It introduces an astonishing, richly-drawn cast of Caribbean characters, starring the street-smart Alonso himself, a most ingenious improvisor in the time-honoured West Indian tradition.

The Macmillan Caribbean Writers Series (MCW) is an exciting new collection of fine writing which treats the broad range of the Caribbean experience. The series offers a varied selection of novels and short stories, and also embraces works of non-fiction, poetry anthologies and collections of plays particularly suitable for arts and drama festivals.

As well as reviving well-loved West Indian classics and introducing unknown work by newly discovered writers, MCW is proud to present new writing by established authors such as Jones, Michael Anthony, Jan Carew, Tessa McWatt, and Anthony Winkler. Writers on the list come from around the region, including Guyana, Trinidad, Tobago, Barbados, St Vincent, Bequia, Grenada, St Lucia, Dominica, Montserrat, Antigua, the Bahamas, Jamaica and Belize.

MCW was launched in 2003 at the Caribbean's premier literary event, the Calabash Festival in Jamaica. Macmillan Caribbean is also proud to be associated with the work of the Cropper Foundation in Trinidad, developing the talents of the region's most promising emerging writers, many of whom are contributors to MCW.

Judy Stone
Series Editor
Macmillan Caribbean Writers

The Macmillan Caribbean Writers Series

edited by Judy Stone

Stories:

1

The Chinaman was more than dead, Alonso thought. He was definitely dead. Lying in that position, his head turned round like a Satanic cat, his teeth bared, his squint eyes closed and an unpleasant substance coming out from where his ear had been, this Chinyman was beyond repair. There was no need for an ambulance or the fire brigade.

The police were another matter, Alonso thought. Something to be considered. He had deep suspicions of the police and hesitated to involve them. The stupid brutes would arrive, all pompous and careful, mindful of procedure, and immediately jump to the wrong conclusion. They would not see it was an accident, they would not accept the obvious, that the Good Lord wanted Chin Lee to spend eternity in those blue silk pyjamas, so he had fallen from the balcony of suite one-one-one and had struck his head on the kerbing, trusting to staff to scrape him off the walkway before breakfast. No, the police would assume that he, Alonso, because he had no fixed abode, no visible means of support, and most important was black and ugly, had done it, had killed the Chinaman without benefit of motive. After all, to arrest Alonso was to solve a crime without the necessity of proof. Alonso decided not to report the matter, and leaving Chin Lee where he was, he returned to the pile of krukus bags behind the spare generator shed to sleep until dawn.

At cock-crow, when the sun touched the tip of the flame of the forest in the patio, and the green lizard took his place on the cotton tree, tail up, head down, eyes unblinking, Carlotta came out for a dip in the pool. It was worth a man waking at six to see that girl in a bathing suit, tanned the colour of nutmeg, thighs like the pillars of the temple, and all the rest of her moving and flowing like music. Carlotta's bikini was cut to the hip bone, and her blonde hair fell to the striped beach towel draped over her shoulders. But peering through the curtains formed by the towel, the lizard lusted only for the freckles between her breasts, waiting for one to move.

Rounding the curve of the raised pool, Carlotta noticed a pile of blue silk among the zinnias, black hair at one end, yellow soles of feet at the other, and she noticed a butterfly, perched on the Chinaman's shoulder, flutter away like a departing soul.

"Oh," Carlotta exclaimed softly, fear disturbing her features, but she looked long enough to be sure of what she had seen, and ran, barefoot, knees twinkling, through the garden to the front office. It was closed. Carlotta went on to the dining room, which was open on one side to the patio garden, and to the palm-shaded beach on the other. It was deserted at that hour except for Precious Ting, putting out the coffee cups beside the stainless steel urn, ready for the guests. Precious Ting was slow, good-humoured and precise, virtues required in one who works all day and half the night. She was scrubbed black and shiny for early morning, and in her neat blue uniform and frilled white apron, she reminded Carlotta of a jade and sapphire bracelet set in silver.

"Mawnin'," Precious Ting smiled, showing perfect teeth.

"Good morning," Carlotta said. "There's a dead man over there."

"Coffee not ready yet," Precious Ting said, thinking Carlotta was boasting about her night's exploits.

"Come with me, I'll show you."

"You serious, miss?"

"Yes. He's over there," and she pointed.

"Oh, Lord," said Precious Ting.

Together, glamour girl and jewel, they approached the body and paused.

"I best wake up Madame Juliette and Mass George. Is not for us to interfere wid dat."

Madame Juliette, as befits the French keeping up standards in faraway places, was already dressed, in the funereal black of the *patronne*, pinning her long hair into a bun. Mass George, her husband, as befits a Jamaican whose bread is buttered, was still in his pyjamas, picking the skin from between his toes.

"What, Precious?"

"One of the gues' dead in the garden, ma'am."

"Which one?"

"The Chinyman in one-one-one."

"Anybody see him?"

"Ongle me and dis lady, ma'am. Dis lady fin' him."

Madame Juliette favoured Carlotta with a piercing glance, deciding she may have been the cause of the death, but not its agent. She turned back to Precious Ting.

"Where's Alonso?"

"Don't know, ma'am." Precious Ting rather resented the implication that she should know where that worthless brute was.

"Find him."

"The coffee cups, ma'am?"

"I'll do the coffee cups. *Allez!*"

Precious Ting, unaccustomed to hurry, tried. Carlotta and the *patronne* went out together, leaving Mass George to pull on his trousers and search for his sandals under the bed.

Madame Juliette, having been shown the position of the body, remembered that Carlotta was her guest, who should not be bothered by a hiccup in the running of her hotel.

"Thank you so much. You must tell me your name."

"Carlotta ... Heneghan-White."

3

"Oh yes, 97. Thank you so much. Run along now and enjoy yourself. Have a swim in the sea. It feels warm in the early morning."

Carlotta was not to be so easily excluded. This was her body, she had found it, and she was going to be involved with it, at least until the mystery was solved.

"Do you want me to call the police?"

Madame Juliette noticed that the flies, little black devils, had found Chin Lee.

"The telephone's not working. A terrorist has cut the line. My husband will go for the police."

From behind the hotel came the grinding of Mass George's starter motor.

The noise did not disturb Alonso, who lay stretched on his pile of krukus bags, Precious Ting poking at his ribs with the toe of her tennis shoe.

"Alonso, Madame Juliette want you."

"What happen? Somebody dead?"

"You know already."

"Know what?" said Alonso, to whom innocence was second nature, trying to correct his first mistake, and failing. "What is the urgency?"

"Just get up."

Alonso did so, shaking the sleep from his head like a dog shaking water.

"Precious, I'm on watch all night, you know. You not suppose to wake me in the day."

"Hurry up."

"If somebody dead, what I business wid it?" Alonso queried, getting to his feet and tightening his belt, which was his equivalent of getting dressed.

"Madame want you to cover the corpse, and to stand watch over it until the police come."

"You has a tarpaulin?"

"Bring de krukus bags."

"This is my bed, Precious. I can't use dat."

"You call dat a bed?"

"Yes," Alonso said, his voice wheedling and tender. "Precious, I could have slumberland if I want. My daddy did dig de Panama Canal and I has boxes of gold. I only sleep on krukus bag so a pretty gal will take pity on me and ask me to share."

"What kinda gal going share wid you? There's a tarpaulin in the laundry."

Alonso departed to fetch the tarpaulin which was duly placed over the remains of Chin Lee, squashing the zinnias around him. A guest, clad in a sort of floral bell tent, and tugging a three-year-old in her wake, passed the tarpaulin, glancing at it without interest and not even seeing Alonso, on the other side of the path, squatting with his back against the wall of the pool.

Alonso shut his eyes against the white cellulite rippling by and concentrated on his own problems. He was a patient man, for patience and poverty are twins, but there were some things he found hard to endure and one of them was hunger. He was always hungry in the morning, when his rested senses yearned for food, preferably for a meal large enough to put him back to sleep in a blissful after-breakfast doze. He could not abandon the mound under the tarpaulin. It wasn't going anywhere, but he had been instructed by Madame not to move, and if so much as a dog put his nose under the canvas, Madame Juliette would raise hell, and he would pay the penalty.

Mass George was a careful driver who boasted that his ancient Chevrolet still had the original shock absorbers. As the road to the police station was composed of potholes scoured by the rain, he would navigate like a drunk and take his time.

Meanwhile, Alonso endured, his nose adding torture to his torment. From across the zinnias, across the office, from behind the bar and the dining room, he could smell what was happening in the kitchen. Hyacinth was frying johnny-cakes, the coffee was made, Jean was grilling bacon and stirring up saltfish and ackee for he could distinguish the aroma of onions and scotch bonnet peppers. Alonso tried to soothe his own agony by sympathy for his fellow man, remembering that Chin Lee would never smell scotchies again, but it did not work. In fact, sympathy made it worse; it reminded him that he, Alonso, would one day face the eternal empty plate, and until then he wanted to eat as much as possible.

The cling-cling that perched briefly on Carlotta's table, cocking its head to photograph her with one yellow eye, had no such inhibitions of fear or retribution. It hopped from table to table in search of crumbs, lord of this feeding station, getting for free what the tourists had paid for, and scorning them. Carlotta ordered the fruit plate and coffee, resisting the delicious bum-broaderners, the succulent heart-attackers and the greasy acne-makers. She sat patiently at a table for two, nearest to the beach, under a coconut frond with a view out to sea. The sun was on the water now, and reflected off the dazzling white hull of Leprosini's yacht at anchor within the reef.

"Pig," she thought.

There was always classical guitar on the tannoy at breakfast, some unknown masterpiece remembered by Madame Juliette from her youth, which the guests accepted gratefully as less irritating than another rendition of *Yellow Bird*, or *The Yellow Rose of Texas*. To the tinkle of the guitar, Fonseca hove into view, a slim brown man like an upright alligator, with a pencil-thin moustache which served only to emphasise the cadaverous quality of his face.

6

"Morning, Carlotta," Fonseca said, with a courtly little bow. "May I join you?"

"No," she said.

"Be like that. No offence."

"Breakfast is not a public event. I don't want to talk, and I don't want to watch you eat."

"You've made your point. I'll see you later."

"She's probably a lesbian," Fonseca thought, "but still worth looking at." He sat behind her, close enough for conversation, where he could see a shimmer of hair through the coconut leaves, a curve of shoulder and the back of a leg under her chair.

"You sleep in the hotel last night, Miss Carlotta?"

She did not appear to have heard the question, so he tried again. "You didn't sleep on the boat."

"No."

"Did you notice anything special last night? Anything unusual?"

"A man was murdered."

Fonseca sprang up and approached her again, circling her, and sitting unbidden in the chair opposite.

"A man was murdered! How do you know? You saw it?"

"I said I don't want to talk to you."

"I know that, but this is serious."

"I saw nothing. Go away."

"How do you know?"

"Go away."

"But Carlotta, you said ..."

"Fonseca, piss off. You are a loathsome individual. You make me physically sick. Piss off."

She must be a lesbian, Fonseca decided, and turned back toward his own table, but he did not get there. Before he sat down, a siren announced the arrival of the police and his curiosity was stronger than his appetite. Carlotta was left in peace to enjoy her pineapple.

There was a contest going on in the front office between Detective Sergeant Swaby of the Jamaica Constabulary and Madame Juliette of the Casuarina Cottage Hotel. The *patronne* was anxious to have Chin Lee removed and the whole unpleasantness hushed up so she could get back to the serious business of earning hard currency, while the detective was just as anxious to indulge his power and employ his skills. He lived on a boring diet of machete woundings and tourists separated from their wallets, so he insisted. In her turn, she protested. She did not want to be accused of obstructing justice, and he knew that she had the ear of the Minister, so they reached a compromise without a loss of temper.

Swaby, a black heavyweight with added fat, carried out a lethargic examination of room 111, which yielded no evidence whatsoever. Then the body, wrapped in the tarpaulin, was carried back to the room and laid out on the bed to await relatives, if any were to appear, and an ice truck to carry it to Montego Bay. After which Swaby took up position in the bar to question the guests. Forced by his duty to keep his jacket on and only to drink iced water, he sweated copiously, dabbing at his face with a handkerchief.

Carlotta came to see him, still in her bikini though she had added a shirt at breakfast time. Her beauty made no impression on Swaby whatsoever. Half-naked tourists were another species to him and did not disturb his libido. His problem was understanding their accents, which was why visitors sometimes thought him slow-witted.

"I found the body," Carlotta confessed proudly.

"That's the first you saw him? I mean, you saw him alive? Yesterday or so?"

"No. I'd never seen him before."

"Okay. What time?"

"About six o'clock. I was coming for a swim."

"Very good. What time you retired to bed?"

"Why do you want to know?"

"I just like talking," said the detective irritably. "I don't business with your business, but what time did you go to bed?"

"Half past one."

"You passed through the garden at that time?"

"I had been dancing at the Disco Grotto and when I got back, I did, yes, I did ..." She bit her pretty lip, "... but I passed by on the other side like the Pharisee. I didn't see anything."

"Well," said Swaby, "we must find the Sadducee and the Samaritan. Okay, miss. Till later."

Fonseca, hovering by the entrance, was eager to be interviewed so Swaby made him wait until he had spoken to a couple from Detroit, two girls from Toronto and an Italian.

"Fonseca, Richard Fonseca, from Ocho Rios."

"Yes, sir. You know something, sir?"

"Nothing definite but I think you should question the watchman."

"That was certainly my intention, sir, but why do you say that?"

"I saw him about four o'clock this morning."

"Most watchmen are asleep by then. Where did you see him?"

"Just where the thing was. He must have been standing right over the body."

"Ah. And how do you know it was the watchman?"

"I saw him pass under the burglar light. A scrawny-looking black man in khaki shirt and trousers."

"Where were you, Mr Fonseca, when you saw him?"

"What do you mean?"

"What was your point of vantage, sir, and why was you out of your bed?"

"I'm in 230, across the patio. I woke with a headache. I must have been drinking bad liquor. Anyway, I got up·to take a tablet and stepped out on the balcony for a breather. I saw the watchman over there where the body was."

"What was he doing?"

"Just standing there. I didn't think anything of it, you know. I didn't know what the man was looking at. At the time."

The detective was still, nodding slightly, and Fonseca thought he might have fallen asleep. Then he sighed and leaned back in his chair, dabbed at his face, took another sip of water and asked, "You're from Ocho Rios?"

"Yes, I told you that."

"On holiday down here?"

"Yes, I'm in the tourist business myself, managing a condo, so if I want a rest I have to get away from Ochie."

"You married, Mr Fonseca?"

"Yes."

"But you are on holiday alone."

"Is that your business, Inspector?"

"Everything is my business, you know. Any girlfriend?"

"A cat don't travel with his own mice."

Swaby sighed again. "I just want to know, sir, whether there was anyone staying with you or whether you were alone."

"That's not what you asked. I was alone."

The detective then enquired of Madame Juliette if he could have a word with her watchman, to which she readily agreed if he could do so in the kitchen as the bar was opening for business. Swaby had no objection and trailed her black-clad hips into the engine-room of the hotel to look for Alonso, who was found sitting in a corner scoffing a plate of callaloo, boiled bananas and shad.

They recognised each other from one time when Alonso was running a racket in the market selling love potions which turned out to be made of coca-cola concentrate and pressed hibiscus. Swaby had had to let him go as he couldn't prove the potions didn't work. Another time he'd arrested Alonso for running a prayer meeting to collect money for victims of racial oppression. Alonso didn't see why you had to be ordained to do that. Swaby couldn't explain it so he had let him go with a warning.

"You're the watchman, Alonso?"

"Yes, sir."

"Since when?"

"Off and on."

Madame Juliette explained that Alonso was not employed on a regular basis as he was too unreliable. He did odd jobs if required and if he could be found. The title of watchman was largely honorary; some would say it was joke as Alonso spent most of his time asleep.

Alonso smiled gratefully at Madame Juliette. She was making him out to be quite harmless, and in the circumstances, the more harmless the better.

"You were on watch last night?"

"On watch last night. Yes, sir."

"Where?"

"Where, sir?"

"Yes. Where? And don't repeat everything I say."

"Everything ... No, sir."

"You watched last night? Where?"

"At the front. I usually station myself near the gate, you see, sir, round the car park and the front entrance, places like that."

"Who came in late last night?"

"Late, sir?"

"Yes, late."

"Ah," said Alonso, scratching his head, "some come in early … but late, Mr Stockhausen, Mr Thwaites and Mr McWaters, and some women. They went out to dine."

"They were the last?"

"Miss Carlotta, the shapey one, come after that."

"Alone?"

"Somebody drop she."

"Who?"

"Not my business, sir. Somebody in a big car."

"Did you see Mr Fonseca?"

"Who is that?"

"A tall brown man from Ocho Rios."

"I didn't see him, sir."

"You stayed out front all night?"

"No. When I reckon everybody is in and the place lock up, then I take a turn along the beach in case of invasion from that side, and then I take a turn around inside, around the patio garden and the pool, to see that all is normal, and then I have a little sit-down."

"Sleep."

"Sleep, sir! No, sir! A sit-down."

"When you took a turn, as you call it, round the garden, did you see the body?"

"No, sir. At that time all was clear, copacetic."

"What?"

"Shipshape."

"Did Mr Chin Lee have visitors?"

"I can't say one way or the other."

"Did you hear anything from his room?"

"No, sir."

"Did you go up there at all, up the stairs, round the balcony?"

"No, sir."

"Alonso, you're lying to me. You saw the body in the garden."

"*Aiee!*" Alonso let out a little moan of pain and rocked from side to side. He was trapped but he had to keep on lying because if you tell the truth to people they will hold it against you. If he admitted to Swaby that he had knowledge of the body, the detective would ask why he hadn't reported it immediately and there was no answer to that. The truth was he had seen a light in Chin Lee's room earlier and had heard voices, but if he admitted that Swaby would want to know who the people were. He didn't know. But if he said that, the detective would think he was lying, protecting himself or somebody else.

"No, sir, Inspector, sir, see no evil, hear no evil. I had no knowledge of poor Mr Chin Lee until Precious Ting called me in de morning to tell me Madame Juliette want a tarpaulin."

"You're coming with me to the station," Swaby said.

"I knew it," cried Alonso. "I knew dey would arres' me. God help me!"

***

With the departure of the body, Alonso and the police, the hotel settled quickly back to normal. Beer frothed in the darkened bar and guests equipped with towels, creams and airport novels pitched camp under the coconut palms. A lone waiter in black trousers and a white shirt drifted among the deck chairs scouting for dehydration.

Closer to the water Carlotta lay prone on a plastic lounger, a G-string hiding her pubic hair, offering her tender nipples to the sun. She was already brown but rituals must be performed and fading tans are boring, like holiday snaps and tales about changing money. Her tan was still a living brown; her whole body glistened with sweat and oil, tiny droplets decorating her like pearls, and collecting in a little lake around her navel. Her front was nearly done; it was time to turn over.

The sun was scarlet through her closed lids, scarlet and gold flecked with green, the colours moving in a kaleidoscope. Cautiously she peeked between her lashes and opened slowly to a brilliant blue. A black johncrow circled. A paper kite like a stained glass window with a tail swooped and cavorted in the freshening breeze. A clumsy paraglider with legs like sausages, yelling as if the harness had done him damage, was carried past, and on the blue floor of her vision Leprosini's yacht floated, immobile, too heavy to be lifted by the inshore waves.

"Pig," she thought.

She would not look at it. Instead she watched the strolling cabaret, the walkers on the Negril beach. God, people are ugly, she thought. The fat ones and the thin, the bellies below the waist, the bellies above the waist, the bandy legs, the hairy legs, the topless and the bald, drooping breasts and tiny breasts, red pates and peeling shoulders, the girls with haunches big enough for butchers' hooks, and the girls with no buttocks at all, men with hollow chests and tufted shoulders, a female in military trousers with one tattooed tit, and a black man with a rolled umbrella, leading a goat on a leash.

Thank God, Carlotta thought, I'm beautiful, but the thought opened a floodgate of self-pity for she was convinced she had nothing else to offer. She was beautiful but forced to make her way in the world on that one diminishing asset, for she was stupid and had no other qualifications. Everyone else wanted her beauty, to use it and consume it. Everyone wanted to touch her, taste her, forget their own ugliness in brief possession of her. No way! She would not give herself away but selling herself was distasteful and destructive. The truth was women were like soap, diminished by use, more slowly perhaps, but just as surely. Besides, as she had told Leprosini, a girl can do better out of promises. Her mother had told her that the more you give, the less you get. The trouble was Carlotta wanted to give, and give everything, but still she lived by promises, wanting to deliver.

Turning again, she saw Precious Ting sitting by the fresh-water shower, head in hands, a picture of weariness or despair.

"Precious!" Carlotta called, and had to call a second time before the maid lifted her head, saw her, and by conditioned reflex rose, smoothed her skirt and picked up an empty tray. Carlotta noticed that she also wiped her cheek with the back of her hand as she approached.

"You want something, miss?"

"What's wrong, Precious?"

"Nothing wrong, ma'am. You want a drink?"

"First you must tell me why you are crying. You are a beautiful girl, you shouldn't have a worry in the world," Carlotta said.

"Police take Alonso."

"Alonso is your boyfriend?"

"Of course not! But I sorry for him."

"Did he kill the man?"

"No, no. Me sure of that. Alonso is not a bad man. Him is a liar an' a trickster, dishonest, an' you has to say he possess of greed and self-love, but he is not a bad man. Him would never kill anybody because he's a born coward."

The girl is in love, Carlotta thought, and offered comfort. "Alonso will be all right. If he didn't do it, they'll let him go. They only took him in for questioning."

15

"They got him now an' they going to keep him, unless they get somebody else."

"Who did it, Precious?"

"I don't know, miss, but we has to find out or Alonso will hang."

2

At the back of the leaf-littered yard was a row of four concrete cells. After the police had beaten him up, just to show they would not stand any nonsense, Alonso was deposited there to consider his condition. His aches and pains were nothing compared to his mental anguish. He had been separated from the soft life at the Casuarina, disconnected from Precious Ting, and was about to be hanged for a deed he did not do. To keep up his spirits, he began to sing a little ditty he remembered from the Mountain Valley Baptist Church:

> Rock of Ages, cleff fo' me,
> Let me 'ide myself in dee ...

He sang until he was thirsty, and there being no water, and nobody to bring him any, he sat in the corner of the concrete cell and stared at the floor, contemplating doom.

At noon the lock turned, the bolts clanged and a policeman beckoned Alonso into the sunlight. Taking him by the elbow, he led Alonso across the yard to the station, where Swaby was waiting for him in his office. The detective was having his dinner, a tray on the desk which his wife had sent down with curried chicken, sliced tomato, rice and yellow yam. Beside the tray moisture was condensing on a bottle of beer. Swaby ate as he questioned Alonso, chewing slowly and with relish while the prisoner stared so enviously only a hard-hearted man could have enjoyed his meal.

"When you first saw the body?"

Against his better nature, Alonso decided to tell the truth. "Before day."

"I know that."

"If you know, why you ask?"

17

"I just want to know if you still lying." Swaby picked up a chicken leg.

"Nothing but the truth, so help me, God."

"You kill him?"

"No, sir."

"He died from a blow on the head."

"I thought the head lick the concrete wall, sir."

"Wood. Wooden splinters."

"Oh my," Alonso said.

"A watchman carry a stick, nuh?"

"Not me, sir. Mass George don't allow it. He says if the guests feel you has to carry a stick or gun, they is not safe. I carry a whistle, an' if I whistle, he turn on a fog horn. All the gues' wake up and the burglar dem scamper like crab on the beach."

"You didn't blow a whistle."

"No, sir. De man dead a'ready."

"You did nothing. Why?" Swaby was sticking the last chunk of yellow yam with his fork.

Alonso swallowed. "I 'fraid."

"Afraid of what?"

"'Fraid of standing right here, sir."

Swaby nodded. "You saw or heard anything in that room?"

"I hear an argument. Some kind of argy-bargy."

"What about?"

"Couldn't tell. Just a lot of bad language I couldn't possibly repeat to you, sir."

Swaby pushed the tray away, and put the bottle to his lips. He drank, and looked more kindly at Alonso. "How many voices?"

"There was a soft bass voice, and another man talk fast, and Chin Lee chopping Chiny."

Swaby's mobile squawked like a chicken and he fumbled for it. "Swaby."

Another indistinguishable voice, muffled by Swaby's ear, spoke, only a few words.

"Yes, yes, yes," said the detective.

The voice resumed and Swaby heard, his eyes on Alonso. He replaced the receiver and turned to the waiting policeman. "Lock him up."

For once in his life Alonso had told the truth and where did it get him? Back in his cell. It was time for more traditional methods, he thought. Scratching his head, he put his brain to work.

When his guard arrived with bread and water, Alonso engaged the fellow in conversation, enquiring after his health, not good, and his wife, so-so, and his children, of whom the policeman was very proud. Alonso was thrilled by their progress at school but worried about their prospects. He asked the man how much money he was paid by a grateful public and clucked sympathetically at the paltry sum. He enlarged on the luxury life at the Casuarina and let the policeman into a secret. There were rackets at the hotel, undetectable rackets, even legal rackets involving hundreds and thousands of Yankee dollars out of the back of the hand. He could, if the policeman was really interested in the welfare of his progeny, he, Alonso, could put something in his way.

"If you know so much, what are you doing here?"

"That is a foolish question, my good man," Alonso replied. "I am here because of your mistake and I am poor because I'm saving up to buy a private plane."

The policeman smiled, a sunrise smile, pink gums and shining teeth.

Next day, Alonso went on hunger strike. The guard found him prone on the concrete floor, his untouched bowl of porridge within reach of his hand, his untouched mug of water catching flies. Alonso was so still he might have died, for he had learned in his adversities how to hibernate, how to slow his functions down to mere survival. His heart beat sluggishly from time to time and his chest rose slowly every thirty seconds. It was a primitive form of cryonics but very impressive.

The policeman was not impressed. However, on the third day Alonso had not moved or spoken or even urinated, so he mentioned the matter to Swaby, who sent for the doctor.

A little cavalcade of caring persons crossed the yard toward Alonso's cell and, as the guard unlocked the door, Swaby whispered to the doctor, "If the man dead, we don't want any mention of blows or bruises on the certificate, okay, doc?"

"Natural causes. Poor people and criminals all die of natural causes."

The doctor entered, sniffing at the smell, and bent over Alonso, feeling his pulse and skinning back his eyes, which were rolled back into their sockets. "Very impressive," he said, marvelling. "It's the most cunning thing I've ever seen."

He put his mouth close to Alonso's ear so there could be no chance of being misunderstood. "Pass me that needle, officer. I'm going to give him an injection in his backside will make the brute dance like St Vitus, you watch."

The policeman handed him the hypodermic while Swaby, in the doorway, laughed.

"Pull his trousers down," commanded the doctor. "You have a towel? This thing usually draws blood," and so saying, he raised the hypodermic like a dagger.

Alonso held on to his trousers and sprang to his feet, reeling back into the corner of the cell. "Oh, Lawd," he cried, "I'm having a terrible dream. I dream they hang me for murder and I'm lying dead and I am innocent!"

"Quick recovery," the doctor said and packed his tools away.

The scam had failed. Alonso languished for another week with no company but the guard, no occupation but consumption and defecation, and no thought but of a means of escape.

On the third day, a bananaquit flew into the cell; a tiny bird, black, grey and gold. It came in between the bars and fluttered around Alonso's head. Alonso flapped feebly at it in case it had come to peck out his eyes. Then the bird perched on the rough ledge between the concrete wall and the timber roof, looked askance at Alonso and chirped. Solitude had reduced Alonso to fantasy, a condition never far from him at the best of times.

"And good morning to you, Mr Bird," Alonso said. The quit began to fly again, circling under the dark roof. It seemed to have forgotten the way out; the light space between the bars through which it came. The more it tried to escape, the higher it flew, for instinct dictated that the way to safety was always up, up into the solid dark. The bird panicked and in its fear battered its wings and head against the wooden sky, stunning itself until it fell a flutter of feathers at Alonso's feet. He picked it up, still warm and quivering, and cradled it in horny hands, careful not to damage it further. The bird's head protruded between his finger and thumb as he pushed his hand against the bars.

"Chi-chi, bird," Alonso said and released it.

On the fifth day he heard a noise he recognised ringing across the station yard. It was Precious Ting in full voice. She had come to visit him and had been denied admission. That much he understood. Angry now, she was telling the police what she thought of them and of the majesty of the law, and detailing the ancestry of Detective Inspector Swaby in particular, which, according to Precious Ting, had been exotic in the extreme. This tirade led to her being ejected from the station altogether but Alonso in his concrete box could still hear every word. She screamed as she was pushed out onto the roadway and her volume barely diminished. She pitched camp on the other side of the road under an almond tree and from its shade hurled abuse at the station all afternoon. Alonso called back once or twice but desisted when the guard rapped on his door with a nightstick. No such threat could silence Precious Ting, who had gathered a crowd of sympathetic witnesses, rendering her immune to police brutality. She yowled and swore and beat her breast, not only in the cause of Alonso's innocence but by virtue of her passion in the cause of all poor, black, wretched victims rotting in jail around this fascist globe.

Then her voice faded, came back in a burst and faded again. It was time to wait on table at the Casuarina.

On the seventh day, Alonso was once more led across the courtyard to Swaby's office. It was a hot day, like every other day in Jamaica, but Alonso noticed the window was open, wider than the last time, not just open top and bottom for circulation, but wide open, the sash pulled up, the louvres folded back against the wall like an invitation. Freedom was a patch of dirty grass, a peel-necked chicken, a hibiscus hedge with a gap in it, a soda bar and patty stand across the road and a misty mountain range far, far away.

"Alonso," Swaby began, pressing his fingers together like a preacher, emphasising, "Alonso, we found out what happened."

"Sir."

Alonso waited, his heart beating again. They had found the murderer and he was to be released.

"You went up to the man's room," Swaby continued, "and gained admission under some pretext or other and hit him over the head with this ..." Swaby produced a wooden mallet, a square block of cedar with a handle, "... hit him over the head with this and then threw the body into the garden to look like a fall."

22

"I do dat?" Alonso asked weakly, knees knocking, and after a week of solitary, not quite sure. "I do dat?"

"No doubt. What I want to know is, who pay you and why?"

Alonso tried to say something and emitted a little wordless squeak, like a mouse facing extinction.

"You're going to hang, boy," the detective continued confidently, "but if you tell us who pay you, it may be thirty years."

There was a knock on the door, and the corporal put his head in. "Sergeant ... urgent matters."

Swaby rose, ignoring Alonso, and went out, closing the door behind him, leaving Alonso with the cluttered desk and the window open to Jamaica a stride away. He listened for the voices in the corridor but they had moved away.

"Chi-chi, bird," Alonso muttered and looked up at the white ceiling. There was a trap door to the roof space just above Swaby's desk and jumping onto the desk he pushed the trap door upwards with both hands, slid it sideways and hauled himself rapidly up into the croaking lizard-and-rat-infested darkness, replaced the trap door and lay still.

Still also, waiting, was the police marksman in the next room, his rifle trained on the gap in the hibiscus hedge, waiting to shoot Alonso as he fled.

Everybody waited: Alonso in the loft, the marksman with his rifle, Swaby in the corridor out of sight, and at the other end of the telephone someone waiting to hear that the case of the battered Chinaman was closed. The murderer had been shot dead trying to escape.

The police gave Alonso time enough, they thought, to make up his mind. They even encouraged him by switching on a captured ghetto blaster, offering music to cover his exit and incidentally to cover the rifle crack, which could not have been distinguished through the racket of reggae, but nothing happened, no target appeared in the gap in the hedge. Finally, the marksman turned away from his window to Swaby standing in the doorway behind him and shrugged his shoulders. Swaby shrugged back and rolled down the corridor to his office.

It was empty. The window was still wide open and the papers on the desk fluttered in the draught.

"Gone."

"How, sir?"

"You were watching the whole time?"

"Yes, sir. But I can't see round a corner. Maybe the fellow just dropped out softly, and went along the wall like so ..." the marksman mimed his version of Alonso's departure, pressing himself against the office wall, skittering sideways like a crucified ballet dancer, ".... and when him reach de corner, him fly!"

The voices carried clearly through the wooden building and Alonso, in the roof space, listened gratefully. He had used the cover of the reggae music to get away from the trap door. The roof consisted of A-frames joined together, making gutters in the space, and he had squeezed from one section to another like a limbo dancer, scraping his ears in the process, and now lay stretched out comfortably between the joists. He could breathe easy and wiggle his toes, for with birds walking on the shingle and rats running races around him, his own movements could not be distinguished.

From their talk, the police presumed he was halfway to Cuba so all he had to do was relax. This for Alonso meant thinking about food. Where was his next meal coming from? He never thought he would miss prison supper. Even a piece of hard dough dipped in peppery oil ...

When he judged in the blackness that it was black outside, for the chinks in the shingles were long gone, the disco at Rock Cove had yielded to the sound of the sea, owls and tree frogs could be heard inland and the policeman on night duty had begun to snore, Alonso crawled back to the trapdoor, opened it and peered down into Swaby's office.

Nothing. All clear.

He lowered himself and a shower of rat shit onto the Inspector's desk, eased over to the window, slid it soundlessly up, vaulted through and ambled off, taking the recommended route through the hibiscus hedge.

Whether Swaby ever divined the meaning of the filth on his desk is not recorded. Alonso was gone, and from being a nobody he had graduated, by way of suspicion of murder, to the status of a wanted man. He was a veritable John Wayne, the Harrison Ford of Negril. They found an old photograph of him pressed in the pages of Precious Ting's Bible, but as it was of a black man, taken in black and white and back-lit, all you could see was an oval head, two ears like batwings and the front teeth with a gap between that characterised Alonso's smile. This snapshot they enlarged and multiplied and pasted all over the western parishes.

3

A copy of the photograph was scotch-taped to the glass front of Chin Lee Supermarket in Dragon Plaza and Alonso, entering by the exit door, did not even recognise himself. "Mistress Chin Lee?"

"What do you want?"

"Talk."

"Who send you?"

"Nobody."

"Go away."

The Chinywoman sitting at the cash register, a tiny little thing with skin like a yellow rose petal and ink-black hair, returned to scribbling in her exercise book. Alonso noticed that she couldn't write properly, she just made marks, and her hand moved the wrong way on the page.

"The police come to see you?"

The scribbling hand paused and a pair of jet black eyes, already narrowed, pinned Alonso against the chrome railing. "Why you want to know?"

"I want to know if they intend to find out anything."

"Who are you?"

"Private investigator," Alonso said.

"Go away."

"You has any objection if I does my shopping?"

"Help yourself."

Alonso pushed against the turnstile, which did not give way as he was on the wrong side of it, and under the Chinywoman's scornful gaze he retreated into the dazzling sunshine of the plaza, occupied by dogs, and went round to the door marked 'Entrance'.

On his left was a stack of rusting wire baskets and ahead the darkened aisles. There were no lights, due either to Chinese economy or a Jamaican power cut. He looked across the table at Mrs Chin Lee, who ignored him, intent on her accounts, though there did not seem very much in the shop to account for.

The shelves were empty except for little clusters of goods emphasising the surrounding bareness. Alonso passed some shining rum bottles, some dusty wine and bottles of liqueur with designer labels. Then after a gap, detergents, and at the far end of the first aisle, a cold display cabinet, warm and unlit, containing three packets of salted shad wrapped in transparent plastic.

Rounding the corner on the way back to the cash register, Alonso passed some canned tomatoes, bottles and bottles of different kinds of hot sauce, some doormats, brushes and some paper cups. He confronted Mrs Chin Lee once more, still empty-handed, but on the right side of the turnstile. "Business not so good."

"What you want?"

"I don't wish you harm. I want to know if the police come to see you."

Mrs Chin Lee remained silent, stubborn and distrustful. Alonso was forced to start again.

"I want to know what you tell dem."

"How much?"

"How much what?"

"How much you going to pay me to keep my mouth shut?"

"Me?"

"Whosoever sent you. How much?"

"Nobody send me."

"Then you're a madman. You come into my shop say you're a private investigator and then tell me nobody send you."

"Who could send me?"

"Them."

"That's what I want to know, Mrs Chin Lee. Who is dem?"

"You're a damn fool."

"Mrs Chin Lee, your husband dead and I arrested for killing him. I don't do it so I want to find out who. I may be a damn fool, as you say, but not mad."

"Why you tell me you're a private investigator?"

Alonso grinned. "Well, it sound superior, and if you tell too many people you're a murder suspeck, somebody going to ring the police and ask if one missing."

Mrs Chin Lee closed the exercise book. She got up from behind the cash register and locked the outside door against the mangy dogs. There was no need to turn off the lights. "Follow me," she said and led the way the length of the market and into a back room, where a few boxes of undisplayed goods were huddled in a corner and there was a wooden table and two chairs. She opened a chipped refrigerator and handed Alonso a bottle of beer. For herself she produced a saucer of melon seeds which she chewed as she spoke.

"Police come. A big fat black man, snuffling all the time."

"Swaby."

"Same one."

"Said he was sorry but the whole thing was under control."

"They arrest me already?"

"Must be. Police advise me to say nothing to nobody because of danger to me and my children."

"You and your children?"

"So him say."

"You know who kill your husband?"

"No, but he was bound to dead."

"Why you say that?"

28

"You see dis place?" She gestured vaguely in the direction of the store.

"Times are bad."

"Yes, nothing to buy, nothing to sell, no money in the community. You know how many children I have?"

Alonso shook his head.

Mrs Chin Lee paused for effect. "Six."

"You're a young woman," Alonso oozed sympathetically. "Six, and no father."

"Me and six children, and hard times. But Chin Lee was going to get rich. You know peaka peow? Chin Lee was peaka peow king. Gambling, morning, noon and night, from blackjack to English racing, and he paid with goods from out de shop. One time he was away for weeks an' I think he was dead dat time for sure, but he come back lookin' like a ghost, wid no blood in his body an' his pocket full of dollars, American dollars! Enough dollars to stock the shop, to make it a supermarket like it say on the sign. But de damn greedy Chinyman gamble it all away in a week. And so it goes for two, three years, an' every time when he get de money, he promise not to gamble it, an' he swear blind and cry, say he never doing it again. Last week he said, 'Stella', my name is Stella, 'Stella, this is de last time, dis is de big scam … we going to be rich an' go to Hong Kong, you, me an' de children, we getting out of Jamaica!'"

Alonso bent his head and scratched his nose to indicate sadness and meditation.

"Out of Jamaica," Stella concluded, "but not to Hong Kong, or to heaven, but to hell most likely."

"He tell you about de big scam?"

"Not a word."

"He tell where he get de dollars?"

"Never."

"An de police say, 'Shut your mouth'?"

"Right."

"So de police is in dis t'ing also. Time to scarper, Alonso boy."

"What?"

"A goin' liff up my heyes to de 'ills, from dense comet' my 'elp!" Alonso said in his best quashie talk. "Thanks, Mrs Chin Lee, thanks!"

***

When the yacht *Swingtime* was at anchor off the Casuarina, and her owner, real estate magnate, film producer and international financier Marco Leprosini was elsewhere making deals, he kept a room at the hotel, number 97. Carlotta used it, for in his absence her duties were diminished and she could not resist the pleasures of a private bath. To sit on the throne without being overheard by Stephen and Selwyn, to stand naked under the shower for as long as she pleased without worrying about the water supply, to walk across the room without holding onto something, and to bounce in bed without falling out added up to her idea of ecstasy.

She was not entirely happy in her work. But it was, she told herself, all that she deserved. She had persistently refused to be educated, driving her teachers into rages expressed by tight-lipped comments, such as "Carlotta has ability but no application", or "Carlotta has leadership qualities but leads other girls astray", or more simply, "Carlotta is a bad student, and a bad influence". When, in the teeth of this disapproval, Carlotta woke up to find God had rewarded her with the sort of looks that made poets despair, feminists furious, yobbos howl and rich men count the cost, she gave up education altogether and threw herself into a chauvinist world unable to type, to file, to perform brain surgery or plead at the bar, totally ignorant of the

Internet and the word processor, a mere comely maiden for the dragon of male domination. It was inevitable therefore that she should meet her Leprosini at a Chelsea party and, impressed by his labels and his credit cards, accept a job as chief cook and bottlewasher on the yacht *Swingtime*, and whatever that entailed.

On the day after Alonso's escape, Carlotta took the dinghy to the boat to clean out the galley and make a list of what she needed if and when they were required to sail.

Stephen, whom she called 'the ginger man' because of his colouring, and Selwyn, of the dark flowing locks and urchin face, who was studying to be a corporate accountant, always stayed on board. Selwyn was convinced that setting foot in Jamaica would give him Aids, and Stephen just preferred to be on the water, even at anchor. He could not live without its motion, gentle or violent, and the comfort it gave him. When Carlotta told him he must want to go back to the womb, he merely shrugged.

"What's wrong with that?" he said.

"Different strokes for different folks," Selwyn said.

The men were drinking Leprosini's beer and watching Carlotta break into a sweat as she counted out the condiments. At that moment, Fonseca, rowed by his man, Bullfrog, hove into view, approaching over the calm sea like a fly walking on a mirror. They helped Fonseca aboard but Bullfrog, not one for conversation, stayed in the rowboat.

"I see you fellows haven't run out of the necessary."

"Not yet. Want one?"

"Thanking you kindly," the alligator said, affecting old-time manners.

Carlotta passed up a cold Stripe to him and another was handed down to Bullfrog in the rowboat, who poured it down his throat in one go, which was his party trick. Then, shipping his oars, he lay down beside them, his feet on the gunwale and a plastic cushion under his head.

"Heard anything from the great man?" Fonseca asked.

"Not a word."

"But he knows what happen?"

"I guess so," said the ginger man.

"Do you know where he is?"

"No."

"The man escaped."

"The murderer?"

"Yes. What do you think of our Jamaican police? I mean what kind of a force is that? They have one prisoner in the station, one man to watch, and they just leave the door open and let him go."

"Good for him," Carlotta said from below. "He didn't do it anyway."

"Oh, she's listening."

"Yes, of course," she said, coming to join them. "He had no motive and George and Juliette swear by him. They say he wouldn't step on an ant if he could help it. I talked to his girl-friend, Precious, and she says he's innocent."

"That settles it," Selwyn said ironically. "What do you expect her to say? Can you prove anything?"

"Of course not."

"So it's just wishful thinking. Female intuition."

"Don't patronise me, you little creep!"

"That's enough," said Stephen.

While Carlotta cooled, the men talked baseball. Fonseca, who went often to Toronto on business, followed the Blue Jays. Stephen was a Dodger fan; his father and grandfather had been Dodger fans. Selwyn followed Milwaukee, for reasons he did not explain. It was clear that the purpose of the conversation was to exclude Carlotta, indeed to drive her away, but she sat, her legs crossed in the yoga position so as to tan the inside of her thighs, breathing deeply and watching the men intently.

"You follow baseball?" Fonseca asked.

"No," she said, "it's like listening to another language but that's fascinating. If you don't understand the words you can listen to the tone and watch the body language. You can learn a lot that way. It's part of the fun of travelling," she added brightly.

"What are you learning now?"

"Mr Fonseca is showing off, talking to Americans about their national sport which he doesn't really understand. You, Stephen, are indulging him, amused, but you're really bored and waiting for him to go, and Selwyn is thinking of something else entirely."

Selwyn pushed his hair off his face and smiled.

Fonseca was furious. The girl was not only a lesbian, he decided, but a bitch. A lesbian bitch! He finished his beer and stood up. "Stephen, a word … a private word. You want to just row out a little ways with us?"

"I don't want to but I will," Stephen said, and grinned at Carlotta. "Mr Fonseca has no secrets, Carlotta. He just doesn't trust women."

"Right," Fonseca agreed.

The ginger man and the alligator were rowed out by the bullfrog toward the reef, to where the white foam appeared and the blue darkened beyond it. Carlotta and Selwyn watched them go and return. She did not want to know their bloody secrets but she wondered what they were.

4

Mountain Valley was supremely unimportant in the history of Jamaica. The Arawak Indians, who liked caves, clay pots and fish, stayed out of it. The Spaniards never found it. In the days of slavery it was thought too steep and infertile for sugar and too far away for anything else. It was finally settled by runaway slaves and those considered too old or weak and therefore freed. A shipload of Germans settled nearby and miscegenated cautiously, for fear of albinism. Mountain Valley flourished briefly in the coffee boom and declined when the soil eroded. It prospered again growing ginger and briefly bananas, cultivated all this time by Alonso's hard-handed splay-footed ancestors, obliging and humorous when fed, red-eyed and murderous when drunk, gentle, superstitious, mad, taking out their anger and frustration on their eternally pregnant and embattled women.

Now all of a sudden Mountain Valley was in renaissance, not just because it was the birthplace of a wanted man but because of a previously unconsidered crop, grown out of sight and valued only by a small group of lunatics so debauched that they forswore honest toil and lived with lice and hallucination. This casual crop had become fashionable in foreign parts among rich people, for the impoverished soil of Mountain Valley grew the best ganja in the world.

The road to Mountain Valley had not seen wheeled traffic for a long time. It resembled a riverbed in places, and in others something engineered by a goat. Alonso arrived on foot. The Baptist Church, he noticed, had a shiny new zinc roof and the big breadfruit tree was blown down. Miss Kelly's Grocery Store still hung on the hillside like a cat on a window ledge, front paws on the road, back end supported on stilts. One day it must go up or down, but not yet.

Closer, Alonso spotted a man sitting on the roadside, a Rasta, with dreadlocks and a headband in red, green and gold. Rising, the man blocked Alonso's way, a giant, six foot seven or thereabouts, handsome as a lion, all hair and teeth, dressed in a stained safari jacket, blue jeans and trainers, and carrying across his body, God forbid, an old Kalashnikov.

"You are Alonso?" the voice was not bass as Alonso expected from his size, but high, lyrical and strained like a bombastic tenor.

"Who want to know?" Alonso replied, not to be intimidated.

"Ras Clawt."

"You?"

"Me."

"Yes, I am Alonso."

"You kill de Chinyman?"

"No."

"I don't mind, you know. You can kill all de Chinyman you want, an' all de red men, an' all de white men too. Killing is not a crime when you has a political reason."

"I don't kill nobody."

"So come," Ras said in a fatherly way, putting a huge hand on Alonso's shoulder, "come drink a tea and tell me all. You safe up here. Police don't dare to come to Mountain Valley. This is the Republic of Jah. Come meet the freedom fighters."

The freedom fighters were lying about in the shade, partaking of the blessed weed. In their midst a five-gallon kerosene tin, serving as a cooking pot, was steaming on a fire. The scent reaching Alonso, compounded of dreams and reality, made his stomach rumble and his brain reel.

Ras indicated where he should sit, on a box far away from the food, and introduced him. "Dis is Alonso, de murder suspeck."

Alonso grinned sheepishly and kept his eyes on the cooking pot. Some noticed him, some grunted, and others, not to be disturbed, continued their contemplations of the dappled shade.

"You want to know who we are?" Ras continued, sitting beside him. "We are the Army of Jah. We escape Babylon; we liberate Jamaica from the Philistine, the slave-driver, capitalis' and whoremonger!"

"Yes," Alonso said, "I hear about you. Is you cut de telephone line?"

Ras, who seemed to have trouble with a runny nose, sniffed and spat. "That's nothing. We going to do somethin' that will be noised abroad, all over de world!"

"The telephone line was a trouble," Alonso said by way of congratulation, and added, "Something cooking in the pot?"

"Destroy property, power station, hotel, burn Kings House ..." Ras's voice went up another octave, "... dat is not sufficien' trouble. People mus' know and hear of the power of Ras Clawt. People mus' die!" he shouted, and *die ... die ... die* came back from Echo Mountain.

"Policeman?"

"More."

"Soldier?"

"More! All dose suppose to die. You mus' kill de innocent! De innocent!"

Cent ... cent ... cent came back across the deep valley.

Alonso looked at the ragged band. "You don't has many guns."

"Plenty coming," said Ras, "and you see dat box you sittin' on? If you open dat box, you see a plastic cover, and inside dat ... listen to me, don't look ... inside dat ... you know de word 'semtex'?" His voice dropped to a whisper, "We gots it from a Hirishman."

36

Forbidden semtex was of no interest to Alonso. He stepped forward to look into the pot but saw one red eye watching him and stepped back again.

The eye belonged to Lionel who seemed to be second-in-command, as Ras introduced him as Colonel Lionel Zed.

"So, you want somethin' to eat, eh? Alonso, my boy, every man's hand is against you except mine. You escape from the unjust clutches of the law. You goin' join us?"

"I could eat and t'ink about it."

"T'ink first."

Alonso sighed, "Is not dat I coward. When I was a boy I kill seventeen men in Barranquilla, but nowadays I don't have anyt'ing agains' anybody. I jus' wan' peace."

"Every man's hand is against you," repeated Ras. "They will hang you for sure."

"Is jus' a mistake. I never touch de Chinyman."

"If you don't fight, you don't eat."

"I'll join."

"You jine?"

"I jine."

"Eat."

Lionel, Colonel Zed, was pouring out the contents of the five-gallon tin, saving the potwater and spreading the solids on a banana leaf. On all fours, Alonso crept toward the feast and settled like the others within reaching distance of the steaming mess. First, a tiny taste of saltfish with much finger-licking. The starch kind – a chunk of breadfruit, a piece of yellow yam – was hot and had to be blown on, cooled by breath and passed from one hand to the other. And then, dis-creetly, for Lionel's eye was upon him, another piece of saltfish, but leaving the best for Ras and for Lionel, the one-eyed man. Alonso, fresh out of prison, ate like a boa constric-tor, as if he would never eat again, cramming the belly full, stuffing himself to immobility. When there was nothing but juice on the leaf, he groaned and was still.

Ras Clawt passed him a pipe, the stem old and well-chewed, the bowl fragrant with the sacred grass. Alonso drew, inhaled and passed it on. He watched the pipe go round the circle. The man next to him was an ugly brute, but each one after that looked progressively better, and by the time the pipe had reached him for the third time they looked like a band of angels.

Such lovely men! Such lovely smiling men! Alonso found himself giggling, little giggles of joy which passed into peace. He was looking at a macca weed between his knees, what some people call 'shame-me-lady'. He broke off a blade of grass, hearing the juicy snap it made, and touched an open leaf of the macca. The plant, assaulted, closed upon itself, furling itself into a roll of green exposing a sharp prickle underneath. Hours later, Alonso's blade of grass touched the next leaf, and a day passed in its folding. Such beauty.

Far away in the mountains, through the curtains of the wind, he heard the call of the unseen solitaire. Three long, low, sweet notes, followed by a trill. He heard the silence in between the notes, the spaces, the glorious nothings begun and ended by the bird, and the slow pattern of the trill, more melody than any human singing. Such joy.

Fighting for freedom. Pure bliss.

***

It was about this time that the crop-duster, commissioned by Magnus Bonanza, Minister of Trade, to spray the marijuana plantations with herbicide, passed overhead, jolting the Army of Jah. It was only on its way to dump its poison in the sea but Ras Clawt decided that they had been spotted and it was time to move camp. Solemnly and in turn, the men pissed on the fire until it was quite out, collected their belongings, the pot, machetes and one or two rifles of uncertain vintage, and set out on the path along the ridge away from the village. Alonso, as the newest recruit, was commissioned to carry the semtex, warned not to stumble, and advised to walk as much as possible in the shade, as nobody knew what would happen if the stuff got hot.

Up hill and down dale in the blazing heat, their arms and faces scratched by twigs and bitten by flies, the Army of Jah struggled on until it reached the first cockpit of the Cockpit country. If the redcoats, in ancient days, had failed to winkle out the maroons, what chance would the Jamaica Defence Force have against an Army of Jah? Even if they brought in the Yanks and sent in the 301st Armoured Tank and Parachute Brigade, it would be helpless, unable to find, much less to kill them.

Ras's hideaway was at the bottom of a depression, the flat floor of a green crater, the eye of a lush volcano. At the bottom of this cockpit was a vegetable patch belonging to a capitalist, and a quarter acre of cannabis belonging to a friend. There was a spring of water, signs of pig on the slopes above, and total isolation.

"This place is okay," Alonso said to Ras, when he had rid himself of the semtex in the shade of a sweetwood tree. "I saw a yam patch on the way down and some cassava. We can scuffle a few roots an' find some meat-kind or fish …"

"Dis is not a hotel," said the big man in his high voice. "Dis is a base fo' de conquest of Jamaica!"

"Yes, is a okay base," Alonso agreed hastily, for Ras had that quality of benevolence and potential danger that makes the true leader, and Alonso knew not to question him.

Not so Lionel with the one eye. He had sweated all afternoon and, with his depth perception impaired, the trek had been hard and he had sprained his ankle some miles back.

"Conquest of backside," he grumbled. "Your mout' an' your arse'ole change place. You fart but you can't bite. You fart about the rivers of Jamaica running with the blood of white an' brown, and how we goin' build Ethiopia in Spanish Town, and peace and love in Montego Bay. You talk, but you can't do it!"

"You wants to quarrel?" Ras asked politely.

"No. I wants action."

"Is fight you want?"

"I don't fight for joke."

"Nor me, an' I warnin' you," Ras shrilled. "You want rule? You want to be general?"

"If de fighters want me," Lionel said in the grip of hubris.

"Who want Lionel?" Ras asked, "and who want me?"

Nobody was quite sure, so nobody said anything.

"Come, Lionel, we has to battle. Put down de machete."

Lionel took a step toward him, the machete still in his hand, his one eye straining, and Ras shot him.

One minute the freedom fighter was limping forward, the next he stopped, dropped the machete, put his hands to his heart, made a funny noise, pitched forward and lay there, head twisted toward Alonso, eye open, looking at him but not blinking, not ever again.

"We are all brothers," Ras crooned. "We are all equal but somebody has to be leader," he said, sowing a seed of doubt in Alonso's heart.

***

Alonso was delegated to bury Colonel Zed, which was not as easy as it sounds. The cockpit floor was made of honeycomb limestone, and the patches of soil were rare and shallow. He had no pickaxe, fork or spade, only a machete for digging and a frying pan for a scoop. Having seen how quick-tempered Ras could be, and not wanting to lie beside Lionel, he persevered until he had scraped a shallow trench, covered the martyr with dirt and vegetation, and weighted him down with stones. Doing so, he remembered Chin Lee in his blue silk pyjamas. Death, Alonso decided, was following him about and he didn't like that. It was such a nothing, death, pouncing on you without cause. Life could be miserable but it was something, and as long as you could eat or love or laugh, it was okay.

"Sorry, Lionel," he said to the vanished man. "Sorry. Maybe next time … maybe never."

By way of reward or initiation, Ras found another task for him. Alonso was sent to liberate a goat.

It took him an hour just to climb out of the cockpit, puffing, panting and streaming with sweat and then he set off toward civilisation, downhill. Soon he came upon a path in the bush which led either to someone's field or someone's hut. Aware that he was a wanted man and a guerrilla fighter, Alonso avoided the path, moving parallel to it through the thick bush.

There it was, through the leaves, a goat – a small tan goat, young and tender! It was tethered by the path, eating every-thing in reach and stripping the bark from the sapling to which it was tied. Alonso emerged from cover, looking around, saw no one and began to untether the beast.

"What you doin', man?"

Alonso jumped. He was sure there was no one there and he had never heard his conscience speak. Then he caught sight of a bare foot and a thin leg hanging from the ackee tree. They belonged to a small boy sitting in the branches.

"What you doin', man?"

"Good evening, boy. I didn't see you."

"What you doin'?"

Alonso never lacked presence of mind. "I notice the goat eat off this section so I decide to move him."

"You business with the goat?" said the boy, swinging down from the ackee tree. He was about ten with big eyes, a shaven head, thin arms and legs sticking out of khaki shorts and a torn T-shirt.

"No, no business, just a kindness."

"Nothing name kindness, man. You trying to t'ief my goat."

"Oh, is your goat!" Alonso said, feigning surprise.

"Yes, my goat. Leggo de rope."

"Your goat, eh? What a lucky boy you are. You can help to liberate Jamaica. You can do something today you will be proud of all your life, something dat will live in song an' story."

The boy looked solemn.

"You know of the Army of Jah?"

The boy shook his head.

"It is a mighty force come from Jerusalem to liberate us all, to bring peace and love and prosperity to all and sundry. You don't know about them?"

"No."

"Are you poor?"

"Yes."

"Are you oppressed?"

"Don't know."

"When you are a big man, you want to be rich?"

"Yes."

"So jine with the Army of Jah. Inves' in freedom. Give us one goat today and we will give you twenty goat tomorrow."

"Twenty!"

"What is your name?"

"Benjy."

"This story will be part of our history. It will be called 'How Benjy saved the Army of Jah'."

Alonso untied the goat and holding the boy's hand he set off up the path.

The freedom fighters feasted that night on curry goat, and Benjy's father beat his son till he was raw but did not persuade him his sacrifice was vain. The boy still waits patiently for his twenty goats.

Alonso did not eat that night. The seed of doubt was growing.

***

The weed had been cut, dried on bamboo frames, minced or woven into ropes, stuffed into sacks, deposited by roadsides or under verandahs in thick shade, hidden in piles of coconuts or in the shells of wrecked and rusted automobiles; it had been headed down the mountains on mule or donkey-back, or travelled incognito in the company of yam or okra or mango or tomato.

The time was ripe and Ras declared that it was time to strike and put in motion Operation Sugar. They moved at night around the western parishes to gather in the goods. Armed with torn and dirty dollar bills, *you-ess*, featuring George Washington, they pressed horny hands and left men satisfied, with money made, no further risk. The risk belonged to Ras and his intrepid band.

The sacks were buried under a load of bananas for their journey to the sea. Ras drove the truck, Alonso riding shotgun as he thought, with three other men stretched out on top of the bananas. They swayed and rattled down the hill and through the three o'clock-in-the-morning-village guarded by starving dogs. They coasted down toward the harbour, brakes squeaking, and found it deserted except for the vast mass of the bulk carrier moored alongside, its decks aglow. The ship, come morning, was to be funnelled full of sugar, the hold showered with sweetness, suffocating rats.

Ras parked in the darkness behind the bulk store, extinguished lights and waited for the appointed time. An hour of silence, of no movement. Then the deck lights went out, the white face of a sailor bobbed up beside the driver's window, and a finger tapped.

There is no siphon built for marijuana, no conveyor belt for ganja, so it was loaded at the double, balanced on the stooped backs of freedom fighters and on the shoulders of the sailors in the know and in the pay of someone. Miraculously, the hatch was open on number two hold and the sacks were lowered to the steel-riveted floor. By mid-morning they would disappear beneath a mountain of brown sugar, to be uncovered where or when.

Ras and the sailor slapped open palms and parted, the white man to his bottle and his berth, the black man to the rattling truck and the safety of the mountains.

Next day they set up ambush on a country road, at a place where the tall bamboos arched, meeting at the top, and lush ferns grew on the high banks – a wet, dark, secret place. The freedom fighters hid among the ferns, conversing in bird calls as the Maroons had done generations before. Two cars passed, filled with Lebanese merchants, then a mule cart and an ambulance, then an overloaded omnibus called Honey Bee. No one moved. They knew what they were waiting for and recognised it before seeing it by the smooth hum of its well-tuned engine. It was an SUV, with the insignia of the Peace Corps painted on one side, and on the other, the Stars and Stripes, driven by Selwyn, the student accountant of the yacht *Swingtime*.

Ras stepped out into the middle of the road. The SUV stopped. Selwyn, the image of Bob Marley on his chest, his urchin face aglow, his tangled locks down to his shoulders, danced around the car to unlock the tailgate. The vehicle was surrounded by freedom fighters. Ras, the warrior, the leader, the maker of the deal, handed out the spoils – an M-16 to each man, with five hundred rounds of ammunition, and for himself a beautiful brand-new grenade launcher.

Selwyn stood beaming by and when the distribution of arms had been completed, "See you, man," he said, "See you around," popped a piece of chewing gum in his mouth and drove away. Ras and his army, to be taken more seriously now, melted into the ferns.

Confident in their new strength, the Army of Jah re-occupied the village of Mountain Valley. Supplies could more easily be found there in other people's vegetable gardens and on the back shelves of Miss Kelly's grocery store. To celebrate, they killed the headman's pig and stretched it on a rack to jerk. A pit was dug, a big slow fire was lit, slices of pork were laid out on a frame under a roof of thatch and the guerrillas took turns anointing the meat with spices as it smoked.

The smell would have woken the one-eyed Colonel Zed if he could wake, and that man's fate was on Alonso's mind. Ras had begun to take a special interest in him, and instinct told Alonso that it was safer not to be too close to some people.

"You thinking?" Ras said.

"Yes, about Lionel."

"Forget him."

"Long time … but … Zed said you don't t'ief nor trade but you does. You t'ief goat and you trade ganja."

"You don't want de gun?"

Alonso had refused his M-16. The others would not be parted from theirs, and automatic rifles hung from the orange trees like fruit. Alonso had given his back to the leader with a bit of unconvincing flattery – "A big man like you can handle two at a time."

"I don't feel comfortable wid de gun, you know. I prefer fight wid de brain, negotiate, as they call it, tell lies and make promises. Now if that is any good to you, I happy to be a freedom fighter, but jus' pullin' trigger don't appeal to me. My hand too shaky."

The argument that he was already a suspected murderer made no impression on Alonso. He was sure he would get out of that one day, one way or the other, and the seventeen slain Venezuelans in Barranquilla had been a passing phase.

"You must fight my way," Ras said, brooking no further argument.

"Right, Ras, right man," agreed Alonso.

"You believe in de cause?"

"Yeah, man, yeah."

Alonso rose to take his turn at brushing the darkening pieces of jerk, and watching the meat soak up the pepper juice. Around him his friends lay sprawled under the citrus trees and there was a cool breeze off the sea. Could life hold anything more? But without the weed, questions returned, unwanted ideas plaguing him like flies. You can't slap an idea to death, the damn things are too quick, too persistent, too shifty. Was Ras's revolution real? Or farce? Did he, Alonso, want a revolution? Would Ras be a wiser man than Magnus Bonanza, or Mass George, for that matter? Would he run a hotel better than Madame Juliette? And what about Precious Ting?

"'Oman?" he said, rejoining Ras.

"Yeah, man," Ras said, with a toothy smile as big as a tiger's. "Pussy."

"In de revolution?"

"Gal don't business wid revolution."

Alonso looked at the automatic rifle cuddled across his leader's chest. "Who we goin' to shoot?"

"Who?"

"Yes, who?"

"Enemies. Capitalis'. Whoremonger. Exploiter. Sodomite ..."

"Hold on, hold on ... who we not goin' shoot?"

Ras was clearly baffled by this line of questioning. "Why?"

"I want to know so I can be on de right side."

"I shoot you if you ask too many question," Ras said wittily.

A why or even a wherefore was forming on Alonso's lips but he thought better of them. "Right, Ras," he said. "Right, man. I jus' goin' to spring a leak."

Alonso moved away leisurely. Passing the jerk pit, his right hand, unencumbered by weaponry, captured a piece of loin. Then at the edge of the circle he bolted, jumped over a stoned fighter, dived under a guava bush and somersaulted, clutching the pork and falling like a rock in a landslide downhill toward the river.

Before the rifles could be reaped from the orange trees, Alonso was gone.

5

Alonso took up residence in a culvert, a concrete drain, five feet in diameter, where a stream passed under an asphalt road. As temporary accommodation it was all that could be desired. The stream, clear and cool, was only a trickle, but provided water for the necessaries. If it rained heavily in the hills he would be carried away in a flood but it was April, dry weather, and the pipe provided shelter. The few fields in the hillside bush nearby were planted with fruit or ground provisions and there was a bull calf tethered by the roadside. Upstream he found a pool with janga in it, and using his shirt as a basket he caught a couple of them, big enough to eat. At night he could light a fire, unnoticed, and roast the breadfruit or ham which strayed into his possession.

The road passing overhead was a comfort too. Alonso did not know where it went or where it came from but it gave him the feeling of being connected to things. Sometimes the odd bus passed by above him, or a truck or two rattled and thundered, their noises magnified in his tunnel, and at night a smart car hissed by him in the dark. But these did not prepare him for the great awakening.

Alonso dreamed he was far out to sea on a black night with golden galaxies, standing in a canoe filled with naked, kneeling girls, all supplicating, thrusting their sloping backsides at the stars when the beast, the whale, black-snouted, rose from the deep, its huge jaws spread wide apart, screaming, and as it screamed the whole world burst and the air was filled with fire.

"Who dat? Who dat?" Alonso yelled.

The sound was going away, and the thunder and the whining reminded him vaguely of Mo Bay Airport, like an airplane landing, going down the runway. Tightening his belt, he got to his feet and, moving to the mouth of the culvert, peered out into the dawn. Down the road, going away from him, was a jet aircraft, two-engined, small enough to land on a road, big enough to spread its wings over people's pasture and terrify the roadside goats. The thing had landed on him, dropped its screaming tyres five feet above his head, and ruined his morning snooze, no doubt about it.

Alonso watched it come to a stop and slowly turn on its own axis, then, whining piteously, begin to make its way back towards him through the dawn. "Swing low, sweet chariot," Alonso said. "My time has come."

So saying, he ducked back into the shelter of his culvert. Crouched, knees behind his ears, hands in the river stones, he listened as the thing grew closer and came to a stop precisely where it had just touched down, on Alonso's pillow, and noisily began the turning trick again.

Then silence.

"Okay, *pasero*," Alonso muttered. "You can't frighten me. I am in a culvert under a deserted road somewhere in Jamaica and there is an airplane over my head. You can't frighten me."

He remembered telling the police that he was saving up for a private plane, and remembered what his granny had told him about telling lies.

"Use the devil's language and the devil will reward you." Too late now.

On all fours, Alonso proceeded to the end of the culvert, and pushing aside the wild ginger on the bank he scrutinised the airplane. It was very close by and very metallic, and one of the engines, like a shark with its mouth open, was hanging over his head. Looking under it, he saw a man in a leather jacket standing in the belly of the plane, pulling out a plastic sack which he threw onto the roadside, went back into his

Jonah darkness, and did the same again, so there were two plastic sacks with Spanish letters stencilled in black lying on the Jamaican roadside. Alonso had not had time to consider what they might contain, when he noticed that leather jacket, who had black hair, very white skin and a moustache, was pointing a hand gun at him. The gun gestured and Alonso rose, like a blossom from the ginger lilies.

"*Donde esta* Chin Lee?" said the leather jacket.

"Alonso, sir."

"*Donde?*"

"No ... Alonso."

"Chin Lee send you?"

"Yes," Alonso lied, thinking it safer than saying the Chinaman was dead, and getting involved explaining things he did not understand.

"Yes," he said, "Chin Lee send me."

"Okay," leather jacket said and put the gun away. "*Ochenta kilos, y miercoles que viene, la misma.* Okay?"

"Okay," agreed Alonso.

The door closed and shortly the engines began their whining, and the volume rose until the whining became a roar and the wind became a hurricane, and Alonso was blasted back into the culvert, his hands pressed over his ears, until the horrendous howling eased away, diminishing as the thing increased its speed, running away down the road until it lifted, just missing a white Toyota van which was coming round the corner, the folding wheels almost touching the shaking roof. Alonso had no time to sniff around the plastic sacks still lying in the Spanish needle so beloved of goats. He took refuge once again. Being mistaken for Chin Lee could be a dangerous business.

He heard the Toyota stop above his head, its engine ticking over, then the footsteps of two men. He heard their voices, the one high, irascible, giving unnecessary orders, the other soft and surly, agreeing and resenting at the same time. He had heard those voices before. The doors of the van creaked open and clanged shut, and the Toyota chugged cheerfully away. Needless to say, when Alonso peeked out of hiding, the plastic fertiliser sacks were gone.

Alonso sat down in the culvert to consider his condition, the thinker between two arches of light. If he went out to the right that would be one thing, and to the left, another; he really wanted to stay where he was. But he had recognised those two voices; he had heard them coming from Chin Lee's room on the night in question. The flying Latin American, whoever he was, also knew Chin Lee, and carried a gun. They were all involved in some devilry, that was for sure, and all in it together. Flying fertiliser two bags at a time was not the way to make money, so it did not take a great brain to figure out there was something else in the fertiliser sacks. Alonso toyed with going to the police.

He would walk in to see Inspector Swaby and say, "Mawnin', sir ... Alonso. Sorry I ran away. The force of innocence pushed me out the window. But now I have information. A drugs-carrying airplane is landing on a road up yonder, and two men, Bass Voice and Chitter-Chatter are collecting cocaine. So maybe one o' dem kill Chin Lee, cause of some quarrel or other ..."

He wouldn't have time to finish this speech before he'd find himself flogged and back in his cell.

Alonso noticed a soldier crab, making its slow way across the patch of soil left by the last flooding of the stream. Its red, horny legs moved in a pattern, propelling the heavy shell it carried. The crab moved a foot or two and then stopped to rest, pulling the claws in, pretending to be an empty shell. Then the legs came out again, the shell was hoisted and the small pilgrim's progress continued towards a destination known only to itself. Alonso took a stick and tickled the crab's legs. The crab turned into a stone, double quick.

"You think you smart," Alonso said. "You think you smart until bird pick you up and carry you gone, and drop you from sky onto a rock, and you shell burst. Then bird swoop down and eat you. Or small boy crack you on a rock and stick you on a fish hook and dangle you in the sea, wiggling your claws, until a jelly eye take notice and you gone."

The crab had come to teach him a lesson. Alonso wanted to hide, to be left alone, to know nothing, but he already knew, he knew too much, and they, whoever they were, would not leave him alone. Sooner or later the hovering bird would pick him up and drop him. Perhaps if he knew more ... if, for instance, he knew the face of the bass voice, and the colour of talking man. He could not live on stolen breadfruit forever.

Alonso tapped the shell of the soldier crab. "Okay, boss, which way out?"

***

Precious Ting slept with her door locked and her blinds closed. Sea-breeze, as is well known, causes rheumatism, and night breeze, influenza, so, unconscious and vulnerable, she protected herself. It took a lot of whispering under the door and tap-tap-tapping on the blinds before she groaned and sat up.

"Precious, is me," came a whisper.

"Oh Lawd, Alonso, I thought you dead."

"A goin' dead if you don't let me in."

"A'right, a'right, a'right."

The key turned, the door opened and Alonso slipped in like a shadow. He stood for a moment, dazed by the imprisoned warmth and the scent of a woman's body.

"I thought you dead. What you want?"

Alonso had forgotten. In her presence, hearing her, touching her, what else could he want? He sat down on the bed. Her voice was wary. "I sleeping, Alonso. I don't want any foolishness."

"Just a touch, just a feel ... Precious, Precious, Precious."

"No, sir. One thing leads to another and when they hang you, I don't want any murderer's baby to born and raise."

Alonso thought she was taking a lot for granted, even jumping to conclusions, but he was in no position to argue.

"You must leave before day, Alonso. Police watching me like a hawk. What you want?"

"They looking for me?"

"Mmm-hmm."

"So, fine. They looking for a meagre black man with bat ears, wearing tennis shoe with a hole cut out for the likkle toe, khaki pants, a cowboy belt, a T-shirt with nothing on it and another shirt over that with a whistle in the pocket. That's what they look for, okay? I know you have the key to the laundry, and I know in the laundry Madame Juliette has a lost and found box, full of touris' leavings."

***

Nobody noticed George Lincoln Birch strolling through Negril Town, for there was nothing left of Alonso but the space between his teeth. He had a fisherman's floppy hat with flies in the brim, a desert camouflage shirt with Bermuda shorts striped purple and pink, white knee socks and cream moccasins. Two cameras hung around his neck and he carried a straw shopping bag with the embroidered euphemism 'Jamaica, No Problem'.

The white Toyota van was parked under a poinciana in a dusty yard not far from the old lighthouse. On the rocky slope behind, someone was building what might become a substantial bungalow. A veritable forest of wooden forms sprouted reinforcing rods, and two men armed with trowels and spirit levels were slapping mortar about. Piles of sand and cement were covered against the rain, and a lorry from Kingston was unloading terrazzo tiles.

"Money," muttered George Lincoln Birch.

He was tempted to ask for a job as site watchman, then he remembered how he was dressed. Across the street, a fruit juice bar offered continuous satellite coverage of American baseball. It was already jammed with college kids, all white, and George Lincoln Birch decided against that too, and entered the Rocky Cove Disco.

Mid-morning, the place was almost empty. A sleepy-looking girl was loading empty bottles into a crate and an electrician was working on the sound system, stringing wires under the thatch among the coloured bulbs to reach speakers hanging on the concrete posts. Alonso moved to the bar and spread himself across three stools, the shopping bag on one, an elegant moccasin on another, and his Bermuda-shorted bum on the third. "Hiya, miss," he said, too loud and too nasal.

The girl ignored him. The electrician ignored him also, which suited Alonso, giving him time to think. He wanted to ask who owned the Toyota and who was building the house, but decided the least said the better. "Hot in Jamaica," was all he could manage, and then, "Yes, sir, it's a beautiful island you got here."

The girl went on loading the bottles. The electrician came down the ladder to test his connections and a blast of reggae knocked Alonso off his stool and reverberated across the Gulf of Mexico.

"Nice," Alonso said. "Great sound."

The electrician spat and went back up the ladder.

Beyond the bar there was a dining terrace, empty, over-looking the sea, and to the right, another with plastic furniture, a place for rum punches, where, after enough of them, you could see the green flash which accompanies the famous sunset. This terrace was not quite empty for there was a brown girl with curly black hair and a truly sumptuous figure, wearing a G-string, standing on the wall in the sun, posing for photographs. The photographer, a skinny Syrian with boots and a beard, seemed torn between her breasts full-face or her breasts in profile, so she was doing a lot of moving and freezing. There was another girl, similarly undressed, lying on her stomach on a towel with a hat over her head. Alonso liked the posing one better. She, amused by the photographer, started laughing, giggling helplessly and spoiling the session.

Alonso decided she was not a tourist but a Kingston girl and inexpressibly wonderful.

Gazing at her, he was overcome with physical sorrow. Here he was, emphatically in love with Precious Ting, only hours away from her bed and her soft skin, here he was lusting after somebody else. It was no excuse that the girl was very well constructed, and laughed as if she loved life, there was such a thing as loyalty, as decency, as honesty. Why should he hate the little insect with the beard, despise his sunken chest and hairy legs, and want to squash him? Alonso decided Precious Ting would understand and forgive whatever he thought or did. That was why he loved her, and as there was no chance of getting near the brown girl, it didn't matter.

Further down the cliff, hanging over the translucent sea, were other look-outs, isolated concrete platforms on the rocks, reached by stone paths, containing tables where you could wait hours for a drink, or order by the dozen. On one of these, a solitary girl in a white cotton sweatsuit, a wide hat on her head, was sitting alone, looking out to sea. Something about her seemed familiar but Alonso couldn't be sure.

"Want something?" said a voice at his elbow. It was the sleepy barmaid, opening for business.

"A glass of water," Alonso replied, for his disguise had not included money.

"What you say?"

"Jus' water. Too early in the morning for champagne."

The girl reached into the cooler for a bottle of Red Stripe and to the rack for a glass. "On the house," she said. "You're pretty."

Alonso favoured her with his best smile. He was beginning to feel very guilty about Precious Ting.

A man came in from the road and passed close to Alonso. Across his shoulders, like a Chinese water carrier, he had a bamboo pole with enormous carved parrots suspended at either end. The man himself was black, squat, and only his mother could love him. He had been squashed by a flat-iron at birth. His head was flat, his eyes narrow and far apart, his nose flat and his mouth wide. He had broad shoulders and a square torso and short bandy legs coming out of his cut-off jeans.

The man nodded at the sleepy girl, appeared not to see Alonso at all, checked out Venus and her photographer long enough to see they weren't in the market for parrots, and wandered down the terraces in search of customers, of which there could only be one, the mystery woman in white.

"You know him?" Alonso asked the barmaid.

"Name Bullfrog," she replied.

Bullfrog reached the platform where the solitary girl sat, spoke to her, and she looked up at him. Even at that distance, Alonso recognised Carlotta. She and the parrot–seller haggled for a while, Carlotta asked questions, and he, at last, seemed to agree, removed the yoke from his neck, laying it across her table so she had a parrot on either side, accepted payment, which he folded and stuck in the back pocket of his jeans, and came up the cliff again, expressionless.

As Bullfrog came past him Alonso hailed him, using his best George Lincoln accent, "Mighty fine parrots you got there, mister."

"Say what?" the man replied in a soft bass voice.

"I guess they're expensive, huh?"

The man was staring at Alonso as if checking his coffin size. Alonso was not to be deterred. "Handmade by local natives, I suppose?"

"You want a parrot?"

"I just might, a little decoration for my house in New York. How much they cost?"

"Tomorrow," the man said and departed.

Alonso went seriously to work on his beer. He had only heard the voice twice before but he was as sure as they was blue that it was one of them in Chin Lee's room, one of them in the Toyota. Now, if the woman down the cliff was Miss Carlotta Something-or-other from room 97, he better converse with her to find out whether she was buying parrots accidentally or on purpose. She would not recognise him. Blackness aside, nobody knows what a night watchman looks like until something is stolen, and he was double protected by his disguise; he hoisted his shopping bag, re-arranged his cameras and stepped out into the egg-frying sun.

Carlotta looked up at him in disbelief.

"Hi," Alonso said, "how're you doing?"

"Fine, thank you."

"I'm not making indecent advances, lady. I just wanted to look at these parrots."

"Do you like them?"

"Pretty, pretty. You just buy them?"

"Help yourself."

Alonso stooped to examine a parrot. They were both mounted on rings like trapeze artists, with the top of each ring over a hook in the bamboo pole.

"If I lift this one off, the other one will fall down."

"Why do you want to take it off?"

"Just to feel and know the weight," Alonso said, stroking the green-painted bird.

"Why?"

"Well … weight is a question of what wood the artist used. Some woods is long-lasting and tougher."

Carlotta held on to one parrot so Alonso could unhitch the other. He held the parrot in both hands like a baby, stroked it to feel the texture of the paint and turned it over to examine the base, all the time observed by Carlotta's increasingly suspicious gaze.

"How much you pay for the two?"

"Why do you want to know?"

"Curiosity."

"Killed the cat. Who are you?"

"Oh, me? I'm just a tourist, businessman, you know, from New York."

"It's the worst American accent I've ever heard."

"Is that a fact?" Alonso asked, straight-faced, "because I was born in Jamaica, right here in Negril. But I left aged sixteen to seek my fortune in the States. That is why my voice goes back and forth, do you see."

"What do you do in New York?"

"I has a small factory, up Brooklyn way, making stainless steel pipes. Do you think this is solid?" he said, tapping the parrot with a middle finger.

"I don't know."

"So what about you?" Alonso demanded, taking the offensive, not wanting any questions about stainless steel pipes. "I have seen you at the Casuarina."

"What were you doing there?"

"Dropping in, having a beer like now," and, playing a trump card, "but you are such a beautiful lady, I had to take notice of you. You came off the yacht."

"What's your name?"

"George Lincoln Birch."

"Perhaps you can help me, Mr Birch," said Carlotta, rising.

The red inflatable Avon dinghy had disappeared around the point, throttling down for a gentle bump at the Rocky Cove landing stage. At the tiller of the outboard was Stephen, the ginger man, with his muscular legs freckled like ripe bananas. Carlotta made her way down to the stage, Alonso following with the parrots. Stephen wordlessly helped her into the dinghy and reached up for the yoke and the carved and painted birds.

"Thank you, Mr Birch," Carlotta said, waving. "See you soon."

The multi-coloured parrots, like dead fish, lay in the bilge of the dinghy, as it turned with a roar and a swirl of white wake and headed back around the point.

***

"Who was that guy?" asked the ginger man.

"What guy?" Carlotta replied, tempting fate.

"The freak in the purple shorts."

"He's the night watchman at the Casuarina, in disguise. He was just giving me a hand."

"Him?"

"Yes, him, but I told you, he didn't do it."

Stephen shrugged, pointed the flat prow of the dinghy in the direction of the yacht and opened the throttle.

The noise made conversation impossible so Carlotta waited until they were on board and the parrots laid out ceremoniously on Leprosini's bunk. "So what's all this about? The bloody parrots?"

"He ordered them. I guess they're a present for somebody. A kid maybe."

"Maybe."

"Believe what you like. Just don't ask questions."

"Why did you want me to pick them up? Why didn't you do it yourself? Or get Selwyn to do it?"

"You were already ashore."

"I see. That man who brought me the birds works for Fonseca, and Fonseca works for Leprosini ..."

"I didn't know that," said the ginger man. "That's new to me."

"Is it?"

Stephen took both her hands, and sat her down, gently. "Carlotta, I like you very much. I don't want you to know anything that might hurt you. Will you trust me?"

"A man's been killed. I found his body."

"People die all the time. This was a Jamaican Chinese that you never knew who probably deserved what he got. Just leave it alone. Okay?"

"Okay, Stephen. If you say so."

6

When the tap-tap-tapping began again Precious Ting was not best pleased, but she couldn't shout to the man to go away because she might wake up the whole hotel, and certainly would wake up Madame Juliette, whose window was across the laundry yard, so against her will she had to open the door to Alonso, who was still incongruously dressed, still wearing his empty camera cases though he had lost the fisherman's hat when he hitched a ride in an open truck.

She shut the door behind him, and whispered, "Go away."

"Where?"

"I don't mind, just go."

"I must talk to somebody, Precious. I mus' talk to you."

"They goin' to hear us, you can whisper-whisper all you like, somebody goin' to listen."

"All right. No talk. I'll just stay."

"In dat likkle bed!"

"I don't mind," said Alonso hopefully.

"That would be heard, that would be worse," said Precious, raising her voice above the noise of air-conditioning units. "When I do dat, I like to make a noise, say *Oi!* and *Oi!* and bawl out when the rapture seize me!"

The thought of that took Alonso's breath away and made his feet tingle. "No talking and no dat. Precious, just come for a walk, we just walk out along de beach. There's a bit of it with no hotel, no guest cottage, no camp, no construction site, just bush and seaweed and such. We can talk."

"Too tired."

"I beg you."

61

So Precious took off her shoes and they sneaked away from her quarters, past the freshwater shower and out along the beach. There was no moon but starlight sparkled on the breaking wavelets coming in; the horizon was light over the sea and the land behind them dark. Alonso tripped over a drug addict passed out in a hole in the sand but the fellow didn't move or groan. They persevered till they found an upturned canoe out of all sight and earshot and sat down in the sand with their backs against it. Eyes accustomed to starlight, he could see the sculptured shape of her cheekbones and tell whether her eyes were kind, or dreamy, or angry.

Alonso told her his troubles, from the culvert to the Avon dinghy, at which Precious murmured, "I know one thing. If it's bad business, Miss Carlotta not in it."

"How you know?"

"Good people know good people."

She was a hard woman to argue with, so Alonso let it pass.

"It's not just police now, Precious. They landing drugs on me head and my life don't mean nothing to gangster man, they kill me for fun."

"Alonso, you're poor and stupid, nobody going waste bullet on you."

"They 'fraid of what I know."

"Who would believe you? Just go away as far as possible and wait till everybody forget. Don't you have family the other end of the island, a wife and three children?"

"Don't joke," Alonso said crossly. "I has only a grandmother in Port Antonio. When wife time come it will be you, only you."

Precious Ting laughed. "You can't get married. You can't buy a suit. You can't get married in touris' leavings!"

"Any way, any way at all, as long as is you," and he put his hands on her waist: a slim, firm waist.

Precious slapped his hands and stood up but Alonso, sitting on the canoe, encircled her hips now and pressed his cheek to her stomach.

Precious looked at the stars in anguish. "Leggo, leggo, leggo, boy," she said.

But Alonso replied, "I want to hear you shout out *Oi!* and *Oi!* and *Oi!* and bawl when de rapture come."

"I talk a lot of foolishness," she said.

He began to unbutton her dress.

"I warn you, Alonso," she said, "you can't handle me. If I get started, I'm savage, you can't handle me at all!"

***

When it was all over, which took quite some time for Precious was as good as her word, it was decided Alonso would keep house under the canoe, which, as it had a hole in the bottom, was clearly no longer in use. Precious would return to the hotel to do the morning coffee cups. She promised she would be his spy, report on Carlotta, the yacht, and any visiting black man answering to the name of Bullfrog.

***

Alonso dreamed he was driving a steam-roller, repaving the streets of heaven which, being made of golden nuggets, compressed easily into a smooth and billowy surface. Around him the celestial city was dissolving into clouds and the steam-roller came to the end of the road, tipped forward and fell toward the sea, far, far below, towards a deep blue rock-ringed hole straight down, down. The airship burst, scattering sailors everywhere, little white sailors with red hats landing in the water, spluttering.

He woke to find the canoe bombarded by a morning shower, the sand around him soaked, the morning grey. He crawled out into the moist world, no sky, the dark trees sagging under the weight of water, and the still sea a pock-marked mirror. Alonso took his clothes off and ran, penis bouncing, into the water; dived, swam two or three exuberant and inelegant strokes and stood up, waist deep in the water to take the warm rain on his face and shoulders.

Coming out of cloud, low down, he could see the executive jet streaking over Bloody Bay, low, looking for land. It appeared going west, then banked south over the reef and came over land again by the lighthouse, travelling west again over the swamps, completing its circle and then slowing, dropped out of sight going in for a landing.

The airfield, a mere asphalt smudge in the scrub, but known locally as Sunset Strip, had a terminal building halfway along it, under the sock. It was a cottage with two rooms and a verandah where one could wait if it rained. Not being an international airport, there was no need for customs and immigration, but the coastguard kept a man there who recorded arrivals and departures, who in turn kept a woman there to cook for him and a telephone to call the police if something seemed out of order.

The self-important jet arrived, whining like a spoiled child and trailing a curtain of spume. A white Toyota van came out of the undergrowth and splashed across the runway to meet it. There was nothing to report about that. The jet was owned by Mr Leprosini, the millionaire, whose yacht was off the Casuarina, and the Toyota van was meeting it. The coastguard man, drinking cocoa, watched three men and a woman get off the plane. The first was Magnus Bonanza, Minister of Trade, a black man with a swelling midriff and horn-rimmed glasses wearing a white safari shirt and rose-pink trousers; the second was a younger man in a blue suit carrying Bonanza's briefcase; then a middle-aged brown lady in a generous floral print, Ms Pearl, who was the brains of the party; and finally Mr Leprosini himself, a Marlboro cowboy in Armani casuals, his lion-skin briefcase with the combination locks hefted in his racket hand.

From the verandah, through the rain, the coastguard man could not see who was driving the Toyota, nor did it occur to him to care.

Precious Ting was on duty in the bar when the party came to the watering hole. Taking her duty as a spy seriously, she noted that the Minister and Mr Fonseca drank rum to show they had the common touch; the secretary in the blue suit had something soft, as did the self-confident floral dress, expressing her distaste for male camaraderie. Mr Leprosini himself had Perrier water with a dash of Angostura and a squeeze of fresh lime. Precious Ting noted he had perfect teeth because he smiled at her and called her 'miss' in a soft, caring, way. Carlotta joined them and Leprosini kissed her on the cheek.

"Carlotta works on *Swingtime*," Leprosini explained.

"A beautiful sailor ..." Bonanza cried and rocked with laughter, "... or engineer?"

"Crew," said Carlotta coldly.

"Carlotta," said Leprosini, "can do everything. She can navigate, repair the engines, cook ... you name it, this girl can do it, and being British, she gives *Swingtime* a touch of class, don't you, sweetheart?" he said, compressing the crow's feet.

Carlotta asked for a gin and tonic.

Precious Ting was on duty in the dining room when they all went to lunch and were joined by two sweating newspapermen who had driven all the way from Kingston and by Mass George himself who was big in the Chamber of Commerce. One of the press had a tape recorder and the other a big old camera with a flash, like something from a gangster movie. They all ate lobster tails as Leprosini was paying, and Precious Ting ferried Chablis wine in ice buckets and lots of water. Leprosini stuck to the Perrier and sat at the top of the table with Magnus Bonanza on his left and Carlotta on his right. He exuded health that man, his lung capacity a wonderful seven hundred, his heart steady at seventy, and his eyes still set at twenty-twenty.

The lunch turned out to be a press conference and Precious Ting, clearing away, got a glimpse of the architects' drawings spread out on an adjoining table and, listening to Leprosini in snatches, she got the general drift. As she explained to Alonso later, the hotel was to have thousands of beds, swimming pools joined together and hanging tennis courts. There was to be a merino and a gulf course. There were to be villas overlooking the landscape. The whole thing was to be built in Florida out of a swamp and transported to Jamaica in jumbo jets. The marvel of it, she told Alonso, was that it would cost nothing, Magnus Bonanza had been very firm on that point. Magnus Bonanza was government and he had patted the American millionaire on the back and shaken hands with him to have his picture taken. Hundreds of Jamaicans would be earning real money. Precious could hardly wait. The bulldozers were coming and everything was going to happen. Around the table, she told Alonso, they all laughed and joked and talked in big numbers, half a million *you-ess*, and a million *you-ess*, and a hundred million *you-ess*. No, they didn't mention Jamaican money as it's not worth a mention.

***

The party over, Leprosini said he would go out to the yacht at six. In the meantime, he suggested to Carlotta, they could go to her room as he had calls to make. The briefcase was opened on one bed and Leprosini stretched out on the other. Carlotta sat on the balcony while he talked to Vegas and LA and London, Zurich and Monte Carlo, discussing what time it was in those places and what the weather was like, telling guys they were having him on and upping the ante, affirming there was no deal but they could come back to him on that, encouraging guys to keep pitching and promising to talk to them soon and one last thing, at twenty per cent it was possible, maybe, but not a penny less.

The ritual complete, Leprosini pushed the glass slider open, framing himself in the doorway. "What's new?" he asked Carlotta, looking at her feet. Carlotta's feet were prettier than the whole bodies of some people. They had the plump roundness of childhood, firm high arches and toes in perfect harmony, well-manicured. They were on the balcony rail, soles to the westering sun, while the rest of the girl hid in the curve of the deckchair.

"Nothing much."

"There's always news."

"We had a murder."

"Oh, yeah."

"Here in the hotel."

"And nothing new? Tell."

Carlotta looked at him, wondering why he hadn't heard about it, forcing Leprosini to improvise.

"A robbery or a mugging? Or a crime of passion? So tell. Tourist, was it?"

"You would have heard. It was a local person, a Chinese gentleman. His head was bashed in. I found him in the patio."

"Why didn't they get rid of the body?" asked Leprosini.

"The police arrested the night watchman but he escaped. He escaped or they let him go."

"Why do you say that?"

"Why did I say that?" Carlotta echoed and changed the subject. "Everybody knows everything around here. I got the parrots."

"Great. Where are they?"

"On board. What did you want them for?"

"I like them. Don't you like them? I commissioned them from a local artist. It's good PR, like I give to the church and sponsor the native cricket team. I figured the parrots would look good somewhere."

"You can put them in your office and teach them to say, 'Talk to you later'."

Leprosini moved closer, leaned on the rail and put his ball-tossing hand on her shin. "Make up your mind yet?"

"What about?"

"Still hard to get."

"If I say no, I'm on the plane to London?"

"Hell, no, sweetheart. You have other uses."

"Let's stick to those then."

"You can't say no to me."

"What do you want me for?"

"Only one guess."

"Get an exercise machine," Carlotta said irritably. "You can bounce up and down on them, work up a sweat, tire yourself out. They don't have menstrual cycles or headaches. You can mount the damn things at 6.05 and get off at 6.15 a better and a wiser man. They don't have children or nervous break-downs, they don't have mothers, they don't defecate or even get drunk ..."

"But they don't taste so good and they don't give you an orgasm."

"You can do that yourself."

"Watch it, you little bitch."

"Let's get back to exercise machines. You can design one, Marco, or better still get someone else to design it. You market it – an exercise bicycle that gives you an orgasm! It would make a fortune."

"So could you, honey."

Carlotta heaved a sigh and got to her feet. "I'll see you later ... in the bar."

"Make sure Stephen brings the dinghy at six."

Carlotta went out and Leprosini returned to the telephone. He had to call Detroit, Glasgow and Amsterdam.

***

In the bar Magnus Bonanza was outlining to the two newspapermen his views on the drug trade. "We must legalise the thing, man. Marijuana is our biggest business, bigger than sugar, bigger than bauxite. Now, if your biggest business is illegal, what happens? You corrupt society, you sponsor contempt for the law, you make honesty a laughing stock and decency a joke ..."

"But, sir, Minister ..."

"But me no buts, boy!" Bonanza exclaimed, for he was well into his rum. "Every man, Jack and Jill is struggling to be crookeder than the next man. What happens to the values of the church, the school, the teachings of our parents? They are not being destroyed by ganja, they are being destroyed by its illegality!"

"But, sir, minister ..."

"We have signs all over the airport telling lies to our visitors. We make an arrest every now and again and destroy a poor man's field or another man's goods, lock up some poor tourist for a day or so, why? Why, I ask you, why? I will tell you why: to satisfy the insatiable demand for hypocrisy in America. We have to pretend we are fighting the drug traffic to qualify for American aid, just like they have to pretend to fight it so they can make more money out of it. You see, America is already a corrupt society. With all the immense resources of the great nation – army, navy, coastguard, police, medical, judicial and so on – you really mean to tell me they can't defeat three or four Colombian gunmen and a handful of drug pushers? They can, but they don't want! They are all in it together, profiteering on the backs of suffering black people, black and white. Excuse me, this is not a racial business ..."

"Sir, Minister, a word ..."

"If a man grows cane, makes molasses, distils rum, advertises it and sells it, that man can hold his head high and go to church on Sunday. It don't matter that there is a drunk in the gutter some place who drank that rum, or me drinking it and talking it to you. That is not the rum maker's business! I want the same privilege for the marijuana grower. I want a Ganja Growers Association, a Ganja Research Council, and ganja taxes: export, import and sales taxes, all of them."

"Minister ... are you yourself ...?"

"Myself what?"

"Engaged in the business?"

"No! Of course not, emphatically not!"

"Minister, the house you are building here, at Rocky Cove, here in Negril ..."

"It's a personal matter."

"Personal?"

"It is for my mother, for her old age."

Leprosini came in and sat down on the other side of the room. The reporter was still trying.

"Sir ..."

"Time you went back to Kingston, boys," said Magnus Bonanza, ending the interview. "All that was off the record," he said handing back the empty cassette from the reporter's tape recorder. "Quote any of it and I will deny it and sue the newspaper. You know what the official position is – we're going to stamp out the drug trade, right? I totally subscribe to that position, and *that* you can quote. But all that is not new. The news, and the reason you are here, is Mr Leprosini's hotel development. It will mean a lot to the island and I want good sympathetic coverage on that. Right?"

The reporters gathered their belongings and prepared to withdraw. Leprosini was having a good look at Precious Ting. She approached and stood before him, holding her tray like a shield. Some guys like chocolate, he thought. Maybe it would work out real good, a real good time, hey, hey! And it would teach that bitch Carlotta a lesson, he thought.

"What's your name, sweetheart?"

"My name is Precious."

"You can have what you want for it. Would you like to work on the boat for a while?"

"I would love it, sir, but I can't leave this hotel. I permanent."

"You only do the bar or do you do rooms as well?"

Precious Ting was no fool. "To tell the truth, sir, I only do what I want. Perrier is your drink?"

She smiled again and stood aside for Magnus Bonanza, coming to join Leprosini.

"What was all that with the reporters, Magnus?"

"They wanted my views on the drug trade."

"Oh yeah. What did you tell them?"

"We should follow the Malayan example and hang the brutes!"

Chuckling, Bonanza looked up at Precious. "We have to stamp out the drug trade, right, darling?"

"You going back to Kingston, Magnus?" asked Leprosini thoughtfully.

"No, I don't think so, not immediately. I want to see how my house is coming along."

"How about a couple of days on the yacht? I don't have to be in LA until Tuesday and I've got a phone on the boat so ..."

"I might be seasick, man."

"She's got stabilisers and there's no sea to speak of on the south side. We can get as far as Bluefields or on to Kingston if you like ..."

Madame Juliette at the cash register was watching Precious pour the Perrier. "What are you talk-talk-talking with Mr Leprosini?"

"He talking to me, madame."

"And why are you walking all the time on the beach?"

"Me, madame?"

"You, Precious."

"Everybody in Negril walk on the beach. That is the sport."

"I saw you going up the beach last night and again this morning."

Precious concentrated on the Angostura and the squeeze of lime, avoiding eye-contact. Madame Juliette made a face and returned to the cash register.

"Don't get pregnant," she advised the open drawer.

***

"Why you eat everything one time? Why you can't save anything for the next meal so I has to keep coming and keep coming?"

"If you have nothing to do, you get hungry," Alonso replied, leaning his back against the canoe, munching the Casuarina's famous lobster pizza.

"Well, I not coming again. You'll have to break almonds and catch fish."

"All right, I'll come to the hotel to eat."

"Somebody will see you."

"No. I come at night and there's no watchman. I know where everything is. All you has to do is leave out food every night. Leave a plate next to the stove on the right hands side. Leave the kitchen last, and you are there first thing in the morning to wash it up. And if somebody catch me in there, nobody is going to blame you."

***

So it was that Alonso was once more prowling the grounds of the hotel at night. Around twelve o'clock he tested the door to the kitchen, pushed it open, tiptoed in and found the food in the designated place, covered against cockroaches. There was a bowl of *vichyssoise* which he rejected, drawing the line at cold soup, but he did justice to the roast beef, best quality, native-reared, and to Madame Juliette's *tarte aux pommes Normande*. Then, feeling like a new man, he went round to his accustomed place at the front of the hotel, saying good evening and good night to arriving and departing guests, reassuring them thereby that he was the night watchman not some burglar or escaped convict.

He had not been there long when he noticed, in a clear space in the car park, the white Toyota van. Alonso drifted gently in that direction, pretending to be invisible, and reaching it, peered in through the passenger window. On the seat he saw what looked like a brochure, its colours washed out in the half light, advertising a high rise condominium pushing its offensive geometry into the sky, finger raised to the great architect.

"That is a clue," muttered Alonso and put a hand through the window. Just then he heard voices and saw the figure of Fonseca, the upright alligator, coming out of the hotel and heading straight for him. The van was in a clear space, well enough lit, and to run away from it he would have to be in the open, so Alonso moved to keep the bulk of the van between himself and its owner, ducking around to the other side, and as Fonseca approached the driver's door, hiding at the back. The engine started, and the van moved off. Alonso heaved a sigh of relief, short-lived, for the van swung rapidly round to catch him in the glare of the headlights.

Before they got to him, Alonso lay down, playing dead, risking being run over. He knew brown people and knew they wouldn't stop to pick up a dead black man. But the van stopped, fixing him in its headlights. Alonso decided that open-eye, open-mouth dead was more convincing than shut-eye dead and composed his face accordingly. Fonseca's legs approached.

"Get up or I'll shoot you rass. You not dead, you son of a bitch, but you going dead in a minute. Get up!"

The voice was high and rasping, the delivery swift; it was the tenor to Bullfrog's bass and Alonso lay there wishing he had never heard him sing.

"I can't get up, sir. I too frighten."

"All right, I'm not going to kill unless I have to. Get up."

Alonso felt safe enough to reach a sitting position, hands over his head.

"I saw you with your hand in my car."

"Accident, sir. I saw something I wanted to read and the light was not so good."

"You wanted to read!"

"Yes, sir. If you have a gun in your hand, you tends to shoot something; if you have a knife in your hand, you cut; if you see something to read, you want to read it."

Fonseca put the revolver in his pocket. "Haven't I seen you before?"

"No, sir. First time in Jamaica."

"Yes, I know you. Turn around. Put your hands behind you."

Alonso spun his bottom in the dust and felt his hands being tied, swiftly, inexpertly and uncomfortably. He made no protest, praying for some soft-hearted American lady to appear and complain about the barbaric treatment meted out to the natives but the hotel stayed quiet, asleep. Fonseca opened the doors of the van, put him in, tied his legs together with a piece of old rope and then blindfolded him.

"Don't gag me, sir, I beg you. I don't like anything in my mouth. I promise not to bawl out."

Fonseca gagged him, pushed him on the floor of the van like a parcel and shut the doors. The engine started again and death by bouncing began.

7

Alonso never knew how long it lasted or what direction they were taking. He knew when they turned off the asphalt on to a dirt road because the teeth-chattering shaking gave way to brief flights with heavy landings on head or hip or shoulder. The only way to stay alive was to relax, so he relaxed. He decided he was weightless, like those astronauts whizzing round the world in forty or fifty minutes, eating chocolate bars and swimming in the air. He'd always wanted to do that because, in space, he could get out of bed and stay there, roll over again six inches above the mattress and stay there all day.

He slid violently across the floor of the van, hitting the crash barrier of the front seat. Fonseca had stopped.

"Rocket landed," Alonso mumbled through his gag.

The man reached over and removed it. "You escaped, Alonso," he demanded, "or the police let you go?"

Alonso was moving his head round and round to find out if his neck was broken.

"How you escaped?"

"Hide and walk."

"No. They let you go to work for them. That's why you were sniffing around my car. Well, all you find is trouble."

"Me, sir, me? Me don't work for the police, Mr Fonseca. I don't actually have anything against them, they trying their best, meting out the law, but the law don't take Alonso into account."

"How do you know my name?"

"I know de name of all de guests. Name and room number."

"What number was Mr Chin Lee?"

"I forget dat one."

"You going dead."

The van went into gear and shot forward again, bumping worse than ever. Alonso, gagless, added his plaintive vocal to the percussion of the vehicle.

"Aiee!"

Bang!

"Ooohoh!"

Crash!

"Lawd Gawd!"

Bellulups!

"Aah! I beg you, kill me now!"

Alonso's wish was not granted; he might have fainted or lapsed into a self-induced coma for the next thing he knew was that they had stopped. The engine noise was gone, the movement gone, and a nightingale was raising hell somewhere nearby. Birdsong or not, he was still lost, trussed and tethered so he wasn't ready to start counting his blessings. Quite right, because the door was yanked open, the blindfold ripped off and there in the half light of dawn was the tall brown man, Fonseca, and the squashed black one, Bullfrog, who put an enormous hand on Alonso's face, turning it for inspection.

"Yes, this the fellow," he boomed. "Same one. He dress up like an idjiot but is him, same one."

Fonseca and Bullfrog withdrew for a private whispered conference, just audible.

"You want me to kill him?"

"This is an escaped criminal. If they find him on the roadside, no problem, the case is closed."

"Give him back to the police."

"No, we can't do that. He knows we were in Chin Lee's room. I saw him. That's why I put the police on him. He knows who we are so we can't let him go. So kill him!" Fonseca said, handing Bullfrog the gun and walking away.

Bullfrog took it, checked that it was loaded, spat and approached Alonso. The unseen nightingale loosed another burst of song.

"You going to kill me?" Alonso said and Bullfrog nodded.

"I beg you, untie me first."

Bullfrog looked doubtful.

"You hear about Piar? When I was in Venezuela, I hear about Piar. He was a black general in the revolution. So they decides to kill him because revolution is all right for white people but not for black people. So Piar say, 'All right, kill me, but I don't want no blindfold, no hand tied, I want to look straight at de gun.'"

Bullfrog untied Alonso's legs and his hands and propped him up in the back of the van with his legs dangling over the licence plate. So far, so good.

"When you fire the gun," Alonso said, "you want me sitting like so or you want me running away? My woman, Precious Ting, would prefer you shot me in the back. She wouldn't want to know I suddenly turn brave."

"You think you smart?"

"I know I smart but is not going to help me. You are the only man who can help me now. You are smart and you are tough, that's why he want you to do his dirty work. Why he don't shoot me himself, eh? Because when you shoot me dead, and police find out, they are going to ask him about it. 'I don't know nothing,' he will say. 'I just went for a little walk and when I gone Bullfrog shoot the man, I don't know why.' The brown man has head," Alonso said, tapping his brain container. "Brown men have head and black people hang."

"Shut your mouth!"

Alonso did as he was told and tried instead to look Bullfrog in the eye. What he saw was pure malevolence, red and steamy, clouded by a pale mist of doubt. It was life or death

77

and he had to take the ultimate chance. "You killed Chin Lee ... but is him make you do it. He make you do it, hit the Chinyman over the head with a piece of wood. But whatever happen, boss man will go free and you will hang ... unless ... I witness for you. I can say, 'No, judge, is not so it go, is de oday man do it! Swear to God! Is Fonseca do it.'"

Bullfrog came slowly to his decision, and even the nightingale had the good sense to wait for it. "I'll shoot you in the back. Start running."

So saying, he raised the starting pistol and fired, and Alonso was out of the blocks, staggering on his cramped legs, reeling from side to side, an impossible target diminishing in the dawn. Bullfrog fired twice for a false start but Alonso declined the offer, heading for a horizon.

***

The sign by the roadside said 'Commonwealth Development Corporation' and gave an address in Kingston. Behind it, somebody had chopped down the forest so the rain had scoured the hillside, and in the thin soil that was left the scrub was trying to take root. Round the corner there was, actually was, a factory, or so it seemed. It was a long rectangular building, made of cinder block and roofed with zinc. Because of the slope it was built on, one end was at ground level, the other had a foundation high enough for cellarage. There was ventilation in this basement area and louvres high up in the walls but no way of seeing in or out. In letters six feet high in different colours of paint running the length of the building were the words, 'Native Artifactory Ltd', and in smaller letters, 'V J Bamee, Prop.'

At the narrow end, Alonso found a door standing open. Inside was an office separated from a warehouse space by a half partition and containing a desk, a chair and a battered safe with a round combination dial. Beyond the office, stretching into the darkening interior were rows and rows of shelving like library stacks, filled with clay and wooden sculptures. There was no one about. Alonso browsed, marvelling. There were owls and there were alligators, male heads and naked ladies, tortoises and fish and giant crabs and many-coloured parrots.

In the farthest corner, near to a locked loading bay, was a trap door with an iron ring made shiny by palm oil, the cement around it cleaned by usage. Alonso looked over his shoulder, seeing nothing but rows of carvings, and listening, heard only the wind in the trees outside. He lifted the trap door; under it he saw the top of a wooden ladder and a light switch. Illumined, the cellar below contained what looked like a baker's oven, a work table littered with moulds, boxes of mysterious ingredients and, in the corner, plastic bags with lettering in Spanish like those that came off the airplane on the road, identifying themselves as fertiliser. Alonso had the strong feeling that the longer he looked in this hell's kitchen, the shorter he would live, so he flipped off the light as if the switch had stung him and dropped the trap door back in place.

Just in time, for from somewhere a voice said, "Who dat?"

"Who dat say who dat?"

"A joker?"

"No, sir, I name Antonio," said Alonso, incognito.

"What you want?"

The voice appeared from behind a collection of inlaid salad bowls; a small Indian of middle years, smelling of khus-khus perfume. This was no doubt 'V J Bamee, Prop.'

"What you looking for?"

"Food and a place to sleep," Alonso replied honestly.

"This place look like a restaurant or hotel?"

"No, sir, but perhaps you could give me a job."

"Job!" said the Indian, kissing his teeth.

"I could perform a job in exchange for a bite to eat," Alonso said, at his most courteous.

"Where you come from?"

"Black River."

"What you do down there?"

"Fish and make fishing pots," Alonso said, trying to disassociate himself from anything that might give V J Bamee a clue.

"And what you doin' up here?"

"I got a ride goin' to Mo Bay but de man turn aside and drop me off … over there …" he said, waving his hand vaguely. "Mr Bamee, sir, my belly tapping on my backbone."

"You can sweep the floor," V J Bamee said. "Come."

He led him back to the office and handed him a broom and a pail of water. "Sprinkle ahead of you as your sweep, otherwise you just raise the dust and dirty up the art works."

Alonso did as he was told, sprinkling and sweeping the concrete floor, making little piles of moist dirt. V J Bamee moved away, taking no further notice of him. Alonso could hear him as he moved among the shelves, counting and calculating out loud. Alonso was impressed. Maybe all the artefacts that filled the hotels, the curio shops and the waiting rooms of airports all came from V J Bamee. Even if they did, he suspected that what went on in that cellar was the point of the whole exercise.

Alonso collected his sweepings in an old bit of newspaper and carried it in triumph to the office.

"Throw dat outside," ordered V J Bamee.

Alonso obeyed and returned to find his benefactor spooning rice from a pot under his desk into an enamel plate. Then he opened a tin of pilchards in tomato sauce, poured the contents on the rice, stuck a spoon in it and handed it to Alonso. "Eat outside," he said, "and bring back the plate."

Alonso took his dinner up the hill away from the factory, found some shade and sat down. V J Bamee's catering was not up to the standard of the Casuarina but he was a decent man, even generous, a man to be cultivated.

"Mr Bamee," Alonso said later, scraping his plate, "you need any more sculpture?"

"I have too much."

"You has too much rubbish!" Alonso said briskly. "I look at all those things and I can do better than that, I promise you. You have ducks in there that can't sit straight, women with their backside in the wrong place and animals that are neither fish nor fowl."

V J Bamee smiled. "Everybody think art is easy," he said. "Every jackass think he can do better."

"I bet you," Alonso said. "Give me a try."

"You make fish pots?"

"My fish pot is a work of art. Give me a chance, Mr Bamee."

"Okay," V J Bamee said. "Come with me." He led him round the back of the factory where a pile of hardwood logs and sawn blocks of various sizes had been deposited in the wet grass. "Take a piece and make something. Where's your knife and chisel? Where's your file?"

"Black River."

"I lend you some tools."

The obliging V J Bamee found a chisel, a sharp knife and a file. Alonso selected a block of bastard cedar and moved up the hill to a shady spot overlooking the factory. There, full of pilchards and rice, he fell asleep and slept through the long hot middle of the day.

When he woke up, he saw V J Bamee coming up the slope toward him pushing his knees with his hands to facilitate the climb. Alonso, under his tree, adopted a sort of yoga position with his hands resting on the cedar block, head lowered, eyes closed.

"Is pray you praying?" Bamee asked.

Alonso did not move, rapt in a trance.

"You don't start yet?" Bamee said irritably, and Alonso lifted his head.

"I asking the wood what it is, what it want to be, what is the secret shape hiding inside. Any fool can cut splinters off and make a pile of shavings; any fool can make a wobbly duck when the wood want to be a rolling horse or a canoe floating in the stars."

V J Bamee was impressed but not convinced.

"You want the sculpture solid or hollow?" Alonso said.

"If you ask a silly question," Bamee replied darkly, "you get your head chopped off."

The proprietor turned and started back down the hill toward the factory, muttering.

Alonso picked up the knife and flicked away a tiny corner of cedar, then made an incision, and another, to create a V-shaped notch, then started slowly to widen to shape his first concavity.

Just then a man came out of the bush, sitting on the hindquarters of a donkey. In one hand he held the end of the halter rope to guide the beast, and in the other a guava stick to encourage him. The man himself was poorly dressed, in khaki trousers with braces, a tattered shirt without a collar, and a straw hat with a frayed brim. A pair of hampers straddled the donkey's back and hung down its flanks. In each of them a statuette which the man was delivering to Bamee. They were three feet high, a pair of Old Testament prophets, carved out of fustic, incredibly hard, and polished to a golden sheen. One prophet, Isaiah, had a hand raised in blessing; the other, Jeremiah, a finger pointed at the thundering sky. Their headdresses rippled in the wind, their eyes gleamed like desert hawks, their long gowns were fluted, draped and gathered, their feet in sandals waited to be kissed.

The man looked down at the shapeless lump Alonso was holding in his hands. "Good," he said, "good. A piglet with a yellow snake squeezin' it to deat'." This man was obviously the real thing, an artist. Alonso had met his type before. The better they were, the more easily they could be deceived and the more readily exploited. A little respect and a little cunning would go a long way.

"Yes, sir, that's right, a pig. And what is your name, if you please?"

"Words and Music."

"You born wid that name?"

"I was born Zephaniah Cunningham."

"I like dat one as well."

"Zephaniah is 'istorical, but Words and Music is contemporaneous, hartistical an' mittical."

Alonso felt he was getting out of his depth and returned to shallower water. "A pig, eh? Yes, I see the pig but is the snake that is baffling me."

"Just look at it wid your spiritual eye."

"Dat one need glasses. I would consider it a favour, Words and Music, if you could show me – just indicate it roughly."

"I don't want to mess wid your creation."

"An honour," Alonso said. "An honour." He held up the block of wood to the eyes of the stranger.

"The pig, you see de mouth open or shut?"

"Open," the man said. "The breath of life escaping."

"Show me, I beg you."

"Hold de donkey," said Words and Music, and sat down, taking Alonso's block of wood and his tools. He stared at it again briefly, turned it round, and then his hands, the chisel, an extension of himself, went to work, chips flying in all directions. Alonso, watching, laughed with pleasure as he saw the pig emerging, and blended into it the shape of the strangling snake, coil after coil tightening until the pig's mouth gaped open.

"You can leave it rough like so," said Words and Music, "or smooth it down. I like it rough, you know – dey call it primitive – but if it was stone, I'd smooth it off. Here."

Alonso took the sculpture in his hands. It was his after all because he'd had the idea. He'd asked the man to make it for him so it was definitely his, and looking at it, he thought it could be improved. He didn't like the hindquarters.

"All right?" the sculptor asked.

"Not bad," Alonso said. "Now what can I do for you? You goin' sell dose prophets to Mr Bamee?"

"Mr Bamee buy all me work."

"How long you been workin' on dose?"

"Two year, three year. Not all de time as I have to cultivate my ground."

"What kind of money Bamee pay?"

"A big price for dese. A big price."

"How much?"

"Ten dollar."

"Each?"

"He wouldn't go so high. De pair."

"I tell you what," Alonso said. "Let me sell dem for you. I'll give you the pig as security." He thrust the pig into the sculptor's hands, unloaded the donkey hampers and, with a prophet under each arm, went down the hill to Bamee's office.

Bamee looked up from his accounts with a disinterest he did not feel. "Those are not yours, Antonio, or whatever your name is. Those are made by Words and Music, Zephaniah Cunningham. I know the work."

"You been robbing him."

"I do him a favour. If I don't buy them, they're firewood."

"How much you sell them for?"

"That's not your business."

"I want a hundred dollars," Alonso said.

"Go away." Bamee returned to his accounts.

Alonso picked up the prophets and started toward the door.

"Fifty," Bamee said without raising his head.

"A hundred."

"Okay."

"Each."

"Go away."

"And I won't tell anybody what is under de trapdoor."

Bamee unlocked the top drawer of his desk, pulled out a wad of dollars, counted out a hundred and twenty and stopped.

Alonso did not move.

Bamee added two more tens. "Take it or leave it. Greedy puppy choke to death."

Alonso deposited the prophets, picked up the money and returned to Words and Music who was waiting in the shade with his donkey. Alonso handed the sculptor forty dollars, at the sight of which the artist's eyes filled with tears.

"You're a good man, sir, God bless you. You can keep the rest."

8

Swingtime was going to sea, purring along inside the long
Negril reef, going south, looking for an opening. Off the port
side lay the long cream ribbon of beach, palm-fringed, with
resort cottages and low-rise hotels peeking discreetly through
the foliage. To starboard, the sea changed from aquamarine
over sand, mottled by the dark clumps of weed and coral, to
navy beyond the reef, flecked with the odd whitecap briefly
catching the sun then sinking sadly away. Further out, the
dark blue shaded into light and castles of cumulus floated far
over the Gulf.

The ginger man, bare legged as always, stood in the bow,
keeping watch for reefs, for though the depth sounder clicked
comfortably away showing water beneath the keel, any
isolated, uncharted growth of coral could make a nasty mess
of Mr Leprosini's investment. Marco himself, honey blond
curls fluttering in the breeze, an Italian silk shirt protecting his
shoulders, and white bikini swimwear emphasising the size of
his genitals, was playing with the spokes of the wheel. Carlotta
came up from the cabin with Perrier water for the healthy millionaire. "Anybody else?"

Fonseca, already feeling queasy, shook his head.

"Champagne?" Carlotta said to Magnus Bonanza, who had
anchored himself in the shady corner of the cockpit, propped
on cushions. He was wearing a landlubber's sports shirt and
trousers, a pair of trainers and a baseball cap borrowed for the
occasion that read, 'Swingtime, Galveston'.

"Too rich for my blood, darling. I'll start with a Stripe and
move on to Appleton."

Carlotta yelled toward the bow, "Stephen, want a drink?"

86

The ginger man shook his head without bothering to turn around and Carlotta went below. She made no offers to Selwyn, the long-haired engineer, who was in the berth reading a book on corporate accounting. Carlotta didn't like him. She had asked him why he'd taken the job on *Swingtime* and he'd said, "Just to keep going", and she'd asked him what he wanted to be, and he'd said, "So rich they can never put me in jail". That gave him an aim in life, emphasising her own aimlessness. But as she got the Red Stripe off the ice she decided she liked Magnus Bonanza. He was a rascal, but he enjoyed being one.

Close to Negril Town the ginger man raised his right arm, Leprosini went right hand down on the wheel and *Swingtime* faced the sea. The first waves lifted her gently into the motion of a rocking horse. Fonseca leaned over the side and everyone ignored him. Leprosini, making for the western point of the island, pressed a button to raise the huge white triangle of the mainsail. There was not enough wind to sail by, but enough to keep her steady in the lazily rolling sea. They passed the markers of fishpots, shoals of empty plastic bottles of tanning lotion, and little patches of weed mixed with the garbage of passing ships. The vibrations of *Swingtime's* marine Honda attracted a family of dolphins who played across her bows and then jumped close alongside to get a better look at Carlotta, who greeted them laughing and clapped her hands. Along the cliffs, naked tourists like sea-birds nesting in the ledges flashed their plumage and disappeared.

"Gives you a different picture of Jamaica," Bonanza said to Leprosini, stretching his legs.

"Yeah. It's a beautiful country. If you guys could get it organised we could make some money here."

"We do our best," Bonanza said. "Angels can do no more. Were you born rich?"

"Hell, no!" the millionaire replied, looking at the sail which had begun to flap. "We were dirt poor. But my dad had the guts to get off his arse, get out of the slums of Palermo and into the slums of New York. My mother worked in a sweatshop, Uncle Ernie drove a cab, Luigi was a bootlegger – anything to make an honest dollar. They knew the secret of success: work hard and give your kids an education. Your kids getting an education, Magnus?"

"I have two at the University."

"That's great. I went to college in California and I got me a fucking education. I found out if you were a good quarterback, you could fuck all the girls, get it? And you could tell the profs to stuff it up their arses and still get all the grades you needed. Extra-curricular, my brother, that's where the action is. What's your salary, Magnus, as Minister of Trade in the Jamaica government?"

"That's a personal question."

"Sure as hell is. But I can tell you something, I bet it can't build a lot of bungalows," Leprosini said, and enjoyed his own joke. "Do you believe in God? I'm a religious man. I believe in a personal God and I honour and glory in his creation. God's last creation was a naked woman, and whenever I see one it affirms my faith in his almighty power. Look at that bitch, Carlotta, is that divine or is it?"

He leaned closer to Magnus. "You can have her on loan ..." he said, and the Minister grinned foolishly.

"Yeah ... college," he resumed. "One of the broads I was exercising at the time became Babsie, my wife. Her father is a real smooth operator, knows everything there is to know about the law but he doesn't think big. I think big, so I went into partnership with him. Somebody said, 'Give the people what they want.' That's bullshit. You tell the people what they want, make it scarce and price it high, know what I mean?

Now there's one thing God isn't making any more of, Magnus, and that's land. People are multiplying all over but God isn't making any more of God's own country. Every Hispanic, black, Oriental or Polack wants his own piece of America but God isn't making any more of it. So that's where the money is – realty – you call it real estate."

Magnus Bonanza was looking across Black River Bay. The water was shallower there, smooth and oily, greeny-brown from the river. The day was increasingly hot. It must be time for a rum.

"Of course," Leprosini said, "you can make mistakes. Some crook can unload a piece of contaminated desert or an apartment block that's sliding into the canyon. You've got to keep your eyes open and know the right people, stay sober, stay healthy and get a tennis coach. Buy cheap, sell dear and guard your back."

"If people want a little happiness, you can sell that too," Bonanza said gloomily.

Leprosini leaned forward and patted the Minister's knee. "I like you, Magnus."

***

Bluefields is not a harbour but an anchorage. A steep-sided mountain thick with bush protects it from the north wind, and a reef protects it from the sea, making a strip of water inshore as placid as a lake. The coast road occupies the space between the mountain and the sea, ducking briefly out of sight behind a patch of swamp where the white egrets nest, making the mangrove blossom in the fading light.

As the birds began to come in, the ginger man dropped *Swingtime's* anchor on the sandy bottom and the yacht settled back for its own rest. Carlotta was busy serving canapés and drinks when Fonseca, recovered, pointed at a dirty grey motor launch chugging in their direction. As it approached, the crew could be distinguished: three men in berets and khaki uniforms carrying guns that looked like modern versions of a crossbow.

"The coastguard," said the ginger man.

"You're kidding," said Leprosini.

"Oh yes," Bonanza said. "We have one. We promised President Bush to stamp out the drug trade."

The ginger man yelled at the launch to back off until he had lowered his fenders, and put the ship's ladder over the side. The leader of the coastguard, a plump young Afro-Indian, had a little difficulty getting on board as he had a radio to carry, a gun and a clipboard full of fluttering forms. Carlotta offered to take the gun and the ginger man gave him a hand up.

Reunited with his weaponry, the plump officer approached the cockpit. The second guardsman, also armed, took possession of the foredeck, and the third stayed at the wheel of the launch. Below deck on *Swingtime*, the student of corporate accounting, tinkering with the engine, ignored the visitation.

"Welcome to Jamaica," said the plump officer.

"We've been here," replied Leprosini. "We've just come round from Negril."

"I am aware of that, sir. We had a report from the airforce."

Leprosini looked at Bonanza.

"Helicopters," the Minister explained. "Two of them."

"If you are going to make Bluefields a port of call, I have to file a report."

"Stuff it!" Leprosini flared. "We made no report in Negril. This is an American boat. I'm on holiday, planning to invest in this island, for which you should be grateful, and I'll go where I please!"

The Afro-Indian was not amused. "You will go to jail if I please and I will seize the boat if I please, so you had best be polite."

The man on the foredeck shifted his crossbow from one hand to the other.

Bonanza thought it was time to intervene. "You are quite right, officer, and to be commended. What is your name?"

"What is yours?" the plump man fired back.

"Magnus Bonanza."

"The Honourable Mr Bonanza? The Minister?"

"Yes."

"Oh Lord, why didn't you say so, sir? Why you let me start to quarrel with the Yankee man? Sorry, sorry."

"So tell me."

"Oh yes. I am Romeo Foster."

"You live around here, Romeo?"

"We all of us live in the vicinity, sir, except that one," pointing at the man in the launch.

"Where you come from, Fergie?"

"Buff Bay!"

"Yes, Buff Bay."

"Foster from St Elizabeth," mused Bonanza. "I know the name."

"The name you know, Mr Bonanza, sir, is Mary Lou Foster," said the coastguard beaming.

"Mary Lou is related to you?"

"My auntie."

"My housekeeper in Kingston," Bonanza explained to Leprosini. "Well, small world, eh? Pleased to meet you, Romeo. Shake my hand."

Romeo did so and shook hands with everybody else for good measure.

Bonanza went on, "Yes, yes ... enjoy the job?"

"So-so. You meet a lot of people, Minister, but you has to be careful."

"Of course. What do you need for your report? I'm just taking a short cruise with Mr Leprosini, just the weekend and back to work."

"Having a nice time?"

"What else do you need?"

"A few details."

Romeo handed his gun back to Carlotta and fumbled for a ballpoint. Embarrassed, he fiddled nervously with the clipboard and the form he wanted came loose and fluttered away into the sea. Romeo swore under his breath. He unhitched the radio and spoke into it. "JCG four to JCG one. Over."

He smiled at Carlotta as he waited, showing a front tooth tipped with gold.

"JCG one to JCG four. What you want, Foster?"

"I just boarded a boat in Bluefields. Everything is *bona fide*. Magnus Bonanza, the Minister of Trade is on board."

"You know him?" queried the radio.

"I know him from long time. His housekeeper is my auntie. You want me bother with the form?"

"Just make a note of the name of the boat, port of registration and owner's name. Over."

"Advice received. Over and out."

"Marco Leprosini. The rest is on the stern," said the millionaire, bored with the whole thing.

"Have a nice evening," said Romeo affably. "Mr Bonanza, good to see you, sir. A pleasure."

Romeo withdrew, reboarded his launch and chugged away.

***

Ignorance is bliss, thought Romeo, but knowledge is power. His wife, eight months pregnant with their fifth child, was beginning to resent his attentions, so that night, after he had eaten, he put on his old bicycle clips, pulled the scooter out of the shed at the back and set off along the coast road in the direction of Bluefields. He was definitely off-duty and carried no clipboard, no gun and no radio, nothing but a pack of cigarettes and a notebook. When he reached the anchorage, he chose a spot close to the yacht where he could see her shape silhouetted and watch the gently moving riding light atop her mast. Nobody would notice the occasional glow of a cigarette and if he felt dozy it would be a neat place to sleep. As he settled down he asked himself, "Is this vigil really necessary?" and the answer came pat, "Yes", for to discover some naughtiness might mean death, or it might mean promotion, and either would be preferable to staying where he was, watching his family and his responsibilities multiply.

The big trucks and the private cars went by all night, keeping him awake. At about midnight, before moonrise, he heard a vehicle squeaking to a stop, and peering over the sea wall he saw, about a hundred yards down the road, by a bridge over a stream flowing into the sea, a light-coloured van. From it, two men were unloading large objects, which could be sacks or boxes, and pushing them into the dark bush by the roadside. Romeo thought he might get the licence number of the van and set off towards it, keeping on the seaward side of the hill safely out of sight. But he ran out of beach and didn't fancy splashing in the sea, stepping on sharp rocks or the spines of a sea egg. Instead, he waited and watched the van drive off.

Two minutes passed and nothing happened. Romeo was trying to decide whether the discovery and seizure of contraband, without identifying the smugglers, would be worth a promotion, when an outboard sounded from under the bridge and a loaded canoe, moving slowly at first, put out into the shallow channel formed by the stream, making for the yacht.

When he got home Romeo took out his notebook and pencil and wrote the date, the time and 'Toyota van ... Marco Leprosini ... *Swingtime* ... Galveston... loading consignment ... suspect drugs ... Bluefields.' He paused before adding 'Very Important Person on board ...'

Then he tore out the page and ate it.

***

Carlotta in her bunk heard the soft bump of the canoe against the hull, footsteps on deck and voices, low and urgent. She heard a thud as the first package landed on the deck, and a noise she took to be the opening of the forward hatch. As a precaution against sleepwalking sailors, Carlotta wore more clothes in bed than she did on deck, so without needing to dress she was quickly out of her bunk, tiptoeing through the cabin towards the companionway.

Leprosini's bunk was empty. Magnus Bonanza was snoring happily, thanks no doubt to the half bottle of Appleton he had consumed after dinner. From the companionway Carlotta could look over the cabin roof to the foredeck. By their movements she could tell which was the ginger man and which the corporate accountant. Overseen by Leprosini, they were receiving cargo from two men in the canoe and passing it through the hatch. She guessed that Fonseca, who slept in the bow anyway, was taking it from them and stowing it away.

Every instinct but self-destruction told her to go back to bed, curl up and pretend to be asleep, but Carlotta had more than her share of the death wish and instead she came on up to the cockpit, rearranged the cushions, put her feet up and faced the black headland to the east. No one noticed her until the loading was complete and the canoe departed. The ginger man, who slept on the foredeck, dropped out of sight, and the corporate accountant, going below, paused to look at her but said nothing, leaving her alone with Leprosini.

"Hi," he said, perching near her, affable as ever. "Been here long?"

"I couldn't sleep. I came up to watch the moonrise."

Leprosini, not usually clued up on celestial events, glanced over his shoulder. There was light behind the headland now. She wasn't lying about that.

"Why couldn't you sleep?"

"The Minister was snoring and you guys were banging about on deck."

"Sorry about that."

She thought he smiled, but he stayed silent and so did she. It was a waiting game, played on a dark, gently moving yacht on a black sea, the unseen moon turning the sky above them pale.

"It's hot," Leprosini said and removed his shirt, breathed deeply, and tossed his curls. Carlotta pulled her knees up to her chest and hugged them, curling herself into a sitting foetus like a snail going into its shell.

"So what's it all about?"

"What, sweetheart?"

"This trip."

"Sure. We got enough shit aboard to keep motherfucking Harlem happy for a couple of days."

She was embarrassed by the prissiness of her own voice and the precision of her English accent as she asked, "Do you ever think about the people who use it?"

"Think? What?"

"What it does to them."

"No. It's their choice."

"Not when you're hooked."

"I don't tell them to get hooked. I'm a businessman. I supply a demand."

Carlotta looked away. The moon was up now, lighting the island and the sea. "What about the real estate?"

"I do that thing. This is just a sideline."

"Does he know?" Carlotta looked toward the snoring cabin.

"He who?"

"The Minister. Is he in on it?"

"Let's say we're just good friends. What're you going to do about it?"

Carlotta put her head on her knees, avoiding him.

"You going to tell somebody?"

She lifted her head, "No, I'm not like that."

"We don't tell tales out of school, huh?"

"We don't," she repeated.

She let her knees go, leaned back against a cushion and let her legs slide away. She looked up at the drug baron, the moonlight in his curls, his torso bare and gleaming. He was godlike, but definitely not a god.

"It's time, you bitch," Leprosini said. "It's time you begin to pay your passage."

"No. No, and you can't make me."

He smiled. "Jump overboard."

I will, she thought, but her body had gone weak and she was helpless, looking up at him as a deer does at a tiger, hypnotised, insensitised for death.

Leprosini unzipped his designer shorts, removed them and hung them carefully on the spoked wheel. He reached forward and took Carlotta by the hair, hurting her, pulling her forward between his legs. "Give it, you bitch, give it!"

Carlotta sobbed and struggled but there was no way, no other way it seemed to get to the end of this, so she bowed her head and waited to take her punishment. She waited. Then she looked up at him and said in her best schoolgirl voice, "Isn't it supposed to stand up?"

Leprosini hit her hard over the ear and she screamed, which brought Stephen out on deck and to the rescue.

***

After breakfast, restored to respectability as ship's cook and unassailable glamour girl, Carlotta sat on the cabin roof with a mug of coffee to watch the shark. The ginger man, who knew the anchorage, told the rest of them the fish was a regular visitor. It was unusual for one that size to come inside the reef but this was his territory and he hunted in it at least once a day.

The shark came quite close, a dark grey torpedo with its blind periscope, then dived. It seemed to swim under the keel for it appeared again forty yards away on the other side and stayed up, fin showing, as it scouted between the yacht and the shore, making a big semi-circle before heading off, going away along the reef.

Nobody noticed the Indian until the shark had gone. He was sitting on the gunwale, water streaming off his skinny body; he was dressed only in dirty underpants, his hair was unkempt, his eyes blood red. Beside him were two young girls, one in puberty, the other a year or two younger, also wet from the sea, but beautifully clean, hair straight and glistening, their cotton shifts revealing the immature breasts of the one, the little swollen nipples of the other, and their slim hips and legs. They had come in the smallest of canoes which was tied to the anchor rope, its paddle in the stern. They had swum the last few yards, and the Indian, who looked too weak to be so agile, had lifted himself on board and helped the girls up after him.

"What the hell's going on here?" Leprosini said. "Get him off."

The ginger man padded along the deck and approached the intruder. "What do you want?"

The Indian opened his mouth wide, displaying tongue and teeth, and pointed a forefinger down the black hole of his throat.

"What the hell does that mean?"

"He's hungry," Carlotta said from the cabin roof, and the dull red eyes flickered toward her, identifying a sympathetic audience.

"I'm not running a soup kitchen. Get him off!"

The ginger man moved closer. "You heard what the skipper said."

The Indian man stared back at him, daring him, pitting his desperation against the easy strength of the sailor.

"Sorry, Sabu. Get off."

The Indian made a gesture intended to be friendly and reassuring, but which was in the event grotesque, a tilting of the head, a contortion of the body, an opening of the hands.

"I don't want to have to throw you off."

"Why don't we just give him something to eat?" Carlotta said, sickened, but the Indian, looking back at her, shook his head and pointed at his palm.

"He wants money."

"He wants money for drink."

"He's drunk already, or stoned. What does it matter?"

"I said throw the stinking beggar off my boat!"

The ginger man reached out to touch the Indian, who nodded toward the two girls and then pointed at the ginger man, making a circle with the forefinger and thumb of one hand and pushing the forefinger of the other through it. "You want?" he said.

The ginger man paused.

The Indian looked towards Leprosini in the stern. "Big boss," he said, "you want virgin?" and the hand came up again, palm up, "Me father. You pay me." He turned to the girls and spoke volubly, in an accent so thick no foreigner could understand. The little girls demurely observed the men in turn, unsmiling, unafraid and uninviting, merely accepting whatever might be their fate.

"For God's sake, give him some money," pleaded Carlotta.

"Throw him off!"

At this point, Magnus Bonanza came up from the cabin, attracted by the babbling of the Indian, a potential voter. "Let me handle this," he said to Leprosini, and moved towards the Indian. The ginger man relaxed, for he did not fancy throwing the drunk, addicted or merely starving scarecrow into shark-inhabited water. He stepped back to let Bonanza take over.

"What are you doing here, master?"

"Business, sah."

"What business?"

"De young gal pretty, eh? Me young gal, me fader. Me can do business. Gi' de white man what him want, virgin, clean. Dey can tek dem an' keep dem till de boat come back or tek dem to America!" He turned to Leprosini. "You want gal fe wash pot, fe clean house, dey don't need money, no money, and dem obliging ..." He looked at the young girls in a paroxysm of love, smiling toothlessly. "Clean, obliging, no money."

He turned again to Leprosini, "But me is fader, so gimme something, ten dollar fi virgin, hundred dollar fi keep dem! Tek dem! Tek dem! I can't feed dem, boss man, I can't feed dem!"

All this would melt a heart of stone, but Magnus was Jamaican born and had heard it all before. He regarded the Indian coldly, and the unfortunate man, realising he was getting nowhere, was inspired to new heights of abuse. "You only work fo' dem, roast breadfruit! Satan cock is a cat o' nine and Satan cock will whip you till you back is fire and God rub salt in your rass!"

He quieted down for one last try. "You nuh wan' de gal dem? Jus' gi me a likkle sometin'."

"That's enough," Magnus said. "Nobody wants the girls, nobody's going to give you anything. Off."

The Indian stared, a picture of helpless malevolence, evil without power, and Bonanza, in control, looked him in the eye, implacable. "Get off," he said and waved his hand in final dismissal.

The Indian nodded to the girls, who climbed over the side and swam the two or three strokes to the canoe. He followed them, climbing in, and paddle in hand began his peroration of abuse, which sounded across the water until he was halfway to shore. Carlotta watched the three pathetic figures, black ants in the distance as they pulled the canoe ashore. They did not go away, they sat or squatted, looking at the yacht like consciences on watch.

There was laughter on the boat and shaking of heads in admiration for the Indian's performance and amazement that anyone should stoop so low. Magnus got himself a rum while they discussed the matter. It was drink or drugs, they decided, or perhaps he was just a beggar, lazy and corrupt, the sort who would not ever work to feed his children or better his condition. The trouble was that with all the goodwill in the world nothing could be done for types like that, for if you gave them money they would only spend it, waste it, throw it all away.

"I'm going ashore," Carlotta announced.

"No, you're not," Leprosini said.

She turned to the ginger man, "Can I have the dinghy?"

"No," Leprosini said. "You're not going anywhere."

"I'll swim."

"There are sharks in the water."

"So?"

"Don't be stupid."

"Okay, there are sharks in the water. What'll you give me if I swim ashore?"

"You want to kill yourself?"

"What will you give me?"

"A thousand bucks. But there're easier ways of getting that."

Carlotta removed the towel draped over her shoulders, kicked off her sandals and dived into the sea.

After the first shock the water was warm. She surfaced and turned toward the yacht, her hair streaming straight, her arms wide, steadying herself. "A thousand dollars, US," she shouted at the men. "You're my witness, Minister," and rolling over she struck out for the shore.

"I'll launch the dinghy," suggested the ginger man.

"She doesn't want you to do that, you'd spoil her scene," said Leprosini. "Leave the little bitch alone."

Carlotta swam steadily on. She was strong enough to make it unless there was a current offshore. She had heard somewhere that sharks were attracted by aimless thrashing, that they would attack anything that seemed wounded but would ignore the regular beat of a healthy swimmer. Whatever she did, she must not exhibit panic. There was no point in looking round for the shape of a fin or looking under the surface through the green glass of the water for the first glimpse of an attacking shape. There was nothing for it but to keep swimming steadily, rhythmically, breathing regularly and deeply. She had passed the point of no return for the yacht was now as far away as the shore. Maybe there was a current, she thought, if not off the shore then parallel to it, for she wasn't making enough progress and she was being swept past the pebble beach she was aiming for and on towards the headland. She told herself to keep going, just keep going. There was no point in swimming faster for that would tire her faster. It occurred to her that she might not make it, she might escape the shark and die by drowning. Her lungs were bursting, her arms and legs like lead, and she began to splutter.

She put everything into a last desperate flurry of strokes, arms flailing. Through a mist of water she could see the shore, a bungalow, a landing stage, palm trees, all bright in the sun. Then the water blurred her vision, she threw her hands up and went down.

Her feet touched sand. That touch gave her hope and renewed strength. She came up, breathed again, and struck out once more, another five yards, another ten. She tried again, touched sand again and waded ashore.

She sat for a long time, head down, arms between her knees. She breathed deeply and coughed up sea water. She rested.

When she felt strong enough, she rose and walked along the littered shore to where the Indian and his daughters sat on a fallen coconut trunk, and sat down with them. They ignored her, for what was there to say? She had been swimming and had brought them nothing. Soon she would go away.

The dinghy and the ginger man appeared from behind the yacht, heading toward her. The distance she had travelled, that had brought her close to death, was nothing to the outboard motor, nothing to the rubber boat skating across the placid calm, leaving a white V-shaped wake, frightening the shark. The ginger man drove the dinghy straight up on the beach, lifting the propeller just before she was grounded. He jumped out holding the rope. "You coming back?"

"A thousand dollars," Carlotta said.

"He sent it," said the ginger man, taking an envelope from the back pocket of his shorts and handing it to her.

"It's a thousand bucks, all right. You can't say he's not a gentleman."

Carlotta looked at the money in her hand. She turned and handed it to the Indian who received it without expression, too stupid or too far gone to know how much it was or what it meant.

"He said to tell you, Carlotta," the ginger man went on, "that if you give it to that son-of-a-bitch, it won't be long before we get it back."

9

The tourist season was in full swing and room 111 – after the Chinaman's demise, a perfunctory search by the police and Chin Lee's lying in state – had been fumigated, cleaned and pressed back into service. The new occupants were a dentist from Toronto and his speckled wife who knew nothing about the murder and, if Madame Juliette could help it, never would. This was a pity for it would have crowned their holiday. The dentist was sexually stimulated by the thought of death, and to help him his wife wore between her breasts a gold heart he made for her from the fillings of the deceased. A cot had been installed for the fruit of their passion, a four-year-old boy, an angel child.

After dinner, it being a fine moonlit night, the dentist suggested an excursion into Negril Town for a drink or two at Rocky Cove and a walk in the cemetery of the old church, if there was one. He fancied it would be populated by clergymen, pirates, runaway slaves and wicked overseers, not to mention women who had died in childbirth or been strangled by their lovers. His speckled wife, foreseeing an exciting evening, modestly agreed, reminding him at the same time that they would need a babysitter.

Precious Ting, washing the last dishes the day and wondering which woman, in which part of the island, was housing Alonso, was summoned by Madame Juliette and despatched to look after the child, Homer.

"You'll have nothing to worry about," his mother promised. "He's had a tiring day, lots of paddling, lots of sun – he'll sleep like a log. Now Precious, what a lovely name, you just make yourself comfortable out here on the balcony. But keep one eye open, just in case."

"Yes, missis."

The wife swung her handbag over her shoulder, letting it rest on an ample canary yellow hip, and set off. The dentist came back and whispered to Precious Ting. "If he wakes, just tell him a story; he likes stories."

"Yes, sir."

They departed and Precious did as she was told, reclining in the lounger on the balcony, pretending to be a guest, bathing in the moist light, scenting the jasmine from the patio garden below, listening to the faraway disco competing with the slow rhythm of the waves.

"I want a Coca-Cola," said a small voice behind her.

The elf had risen, pyjama child, barefooted, and had sneaked up before she was aware. "I want a Coca-Cola," the boy repeated in a tone of wistful wheedling that reminded her of Alonso at his worst. "If you're the babysitter, you must do what I say," the child went on, showing an early grasp of neo-colonialist logic.

"You want ice?"

"Of course."

Precious rose, went downstairs and made her way across the scented patio to the bar, got him a Coca-Cola debited to room 111, and returned to find all the lights on and the child propped up by pillows on one of the twin beds, waiting. He took the Coca-Cola in both hands, drank some and, still holding it with two hands, turned his whole body to put it carefully down on the bedside table. "Tell me a story," he said.

"What kind of story?"

"A bedtime story."

"In Jamaica," Precious said, "stories is about animals."

"That's okay."

"Once upon a time," Precious began, "up in the forest, up at the top of the mountain lived a spider – a big spider, enormous, so big!" spreading her arms like wings, "so big and black they call him Grandpa Spider ..."

The little boy's eyes were wide with joy.

"He was so big and strong he could catch doctor birds and eat dem. You know doctor bird?"

"No," said the child.

"Is a 'umming-bird with long coat tail. Grandpa Spider was swiff enough to catch dem an' eat dem."

The small boy looked at his Coca-Cola, changed his mind and said, "Go on."

"Well, sir, Grandpa Spider was de granddaddy of all de spiders in de world and one day he said, 'I know what, I'll ask dem all to a party, all de spiders, an' I'll catch a doctor bird and we'll roast him an' eat him.'"

"Yes," said the little boy.

"So they come, they come to the great forest at the top of the mountain in Jamaica, all de spidah dem from all over the world; yellow spider, red spider, brown spider, white spider, all of dem, and dey came to Grandpa Spider's party. You sure you don't want to go to sleep?"

Homer shook his head.

"Okay, so Grandpa Spider sat in de top of de tree and look down at all of dem, millions of dem, thousands, all making webs, webs like wheel, webs like rope, webs like parachute. De Water Spider found a pool, de Trap Door Spider dug a hole, there was spiders jumpin', spiders flyin' everywhere, laughin' an' singin' and eating one another."

The little boy laughed, "Eating one another?"

"But of course," Precious said. "They do dat."

The boy reached for his Coca-Cola with one hand and the glass slipped from his tiny fingers, dousing the sheets in red-brown bubbly liquid and small islands of melting ice. "Oh-oh," he said.

Precious put her hands under his armpits, swung him onto the other bed and set about repairing the damage. Swiftly she stripped the sheets, bundled them up and put them by the door. "Don't you worry," she said to the mortified child. "No problem, no problem."

Thinking the liquid might have seeped through to the mattress, Precious flipped it over to remake it on the other side. There on the underside was a brown manila envelope, six by four, attached to the mattress by masking tape. She removed it, thinking it would be uncomfortable for the dentist to sleep on, put it with the soiled linen, and in a matter of moments she had remade the bed with fresh sheets from the cupboard.

"No problem," she said.

"You're pretty," Homer said. "I like you."

"Well, a'right," chanted Precious, smiling, "I'm goin' to wait for you," and plopped him back on his pillows.

"Tell me about the spiders."

"Well ..." Precious said, "... there was one spider kept all to herself – a small, slow spider, weaving a thick cross-stitch web. None of de oder spider come near to her. She had a bright red mark, just here ..." touching her stomach, "... an' she was deadly poison. She name de Black Widow Spider."

"'So,' Grandpa Spider said, 'why you stay by yourself? Come jine de party.' And she just turn up her nose and look de other way. So he had was to go down de tree an' talk to her. Now, Grandpa Spider was getting old and though he had eight legs, not all of dem was working, so he took a long time, hobble-de-hobble-de-hobble. But he reach the Black Widow at last an' he says, 'You are not enjoyin' the party?' and she say, 'No,' and he say, 'Why?' and she say, 'Because you don't produce what you promise.'"

"A humming-bird," Homer said, "he promised them a humming-bird."

107

"Dat's right," Precious said and gave him a quick hug. "Poor old Grandpa Spider. He was too old and too slow to catch a bird any more and so he said, 'Sorry, sorry, but everyone will just have to eat what dey can find, ant and fly and suchlike.'"

"'Better than dat!' said Black Widow and she bit him! Deadly poison! And he died. An' all de oder spidahs eat him, piece by piece."

"What are you telling my child?" came a strangled voice from the doorway. There stood the speckled wife, distraught, with the dentist looming over her.

"The poor kid, he's terrified."

Homer was indeed shaken, not by the story but by the sudden appearance of his parents.

"Just a story, missis," said Precious. "A Jamaica story."

"It sounded horrible, terrible, macabre! I'll report this to the manageress in the morning."

"No, Mama," Homer said.

The dentist, unflappable in a crisis, came to the rescue. "Children's stories must have a happy ending," he explained to Precious.

"But yes," Precious said, "it has."

"It didn't sound happy to me."

"I did not finish, sir. The story go, 'and all de other spiders eat him, piece by piece, an' dey live happy ever after.'"

She gathered up the soiled linen and the manila envelope concealed inside, wished them goodnight and departed.

"I'll pay you tomorrow," the dentist called.

***

Precious was in such a rage she couldn't sleep. White people were the cause. How could they be so stupid! If everything had to have a happy ending, if white children's heads were stuffed with happy endings, no wonder they were mad when they grew up, travelled with suitcases full of pills, drank so much

108

liquor and got ugly and bitter and wrinkled and cold, waiting for a happy ending. The fact of the matter was that happy endings were like Christmas, once a year. In between time was hunger, headache and heartache and not much else. You had to teach children to laugh and to scuffle but expect to lose, because winning was extra, next time, round the corner, by and by.

Now that damn rascal was tapping on the window again. First the little tap-tap that said, 'Don't frighten, listen,' then the second tap-tap, little louder, that said, 'Somebody outside, is me, Alonso,' then the third tap-tap saying, 'Wake up! Precious, it's me! Alonso!'

She opened the door and Alonso slipped in like a cat into a pantry. She made sure he didn't get started on that hugging again because she wanted to get one or two things settled first, like, "Where you comin' from now?"

"Bush."

"Dere's a woman name Bush?"

"No, no, darlin'," Alonso said, in real pain that he should be so suspected, "I was kidnapped."

Precious had to laugh. Alonso being arrested was perfectly understandable but who would want to kidnap him?"

So he told the story of his abduction by Fonseca, his escape from death at the hands of Bullfrog and his discoveries at the emporium of V J Bamee.

She listened, paying him the compliment of credence, and then said, "I was in one-one-one tonight."

"Hmm-hm?"

"Caring for a child. Look what I find under de mattress."

"You open it?"

"No."

So they opened it, moved the contents under the bedside light and looked at them together. There was a red, white and blue British Airways ticket and a Canadian passport in the name of John Yap Sing.

"Dis belong to a different man, somebody name Yap Sing."

Precious put her finger on the photo. "Different man, Alonso, but is de same face. Chin Lee."

"Chinyman all look alike, you know, an' is a bad photograph."

"You saw de man alive and dead. Look again."

Alonso focused in the light of the fifteen-watt bulb which was all Mass George supplied, not expecting his staff to do much reading in bed. "Yes, is Chin Lee."

"So de passport not real. Forgery! An' de ticket is for de same man – John Yap Sing."

"But Precious, dis man is Canadian. Chin Lee was a Jamaican."

"Forgery! De man was scheming to go to Canada an' disappear, mos' likely wid a lot o' money. Somebody find out, kill him and take de money. Open an' shut case," said Precious Ting, detective.

Alonso contemplated her with intense admiration, not just the golden light on her smooth black skin, or her serious face, or her finger moving over the small print on the ticket, but her brain. A straight brain in a curvy body, he thought, it was the whole point of creation.

The man was running to Toronto, Precious said, "… wid de money, so they kill him."

***

"You want to know who kill Chin Lee?"

"You want to tell me?" Swaby asked, looking into the darkness.

He was sitting on his verandah as he was wont to do of an evening, in his pyjamas, the jacket unbuttoned so his left hand could stroke his rounded belly while his right hand

110

gripped his last beer bottle of the day. His feet were up on the rail, the evening breeze cool on their soles and filtering between his toes as they stretched and wiggled. It was Swaby's principal pleasure and he did not really appreciate voices in his garden; voices talking business after hours. The light was on behind him in the house, moths battering themselves to death on the shade, but even with its aid he could not distinguish the shape of the woman hidden in the croton bush.

"You want to know about Chin Lee?"

"Who wants to tell me?"

"That don't matter. Trut' is trut'."

"What's going on out there?" Swaby's wife said from the dark bedroom where she lay under the mosquito net.

"Nothing."

"How you mean, nothing? I hear you talking to a woman. You have a woman out there?"

"No. This is police business."

His wife was quiet, holding her breath in her anxiety to listen.

Swaby on the verandah leaned toward the croton bush. "What you want to tell me?"

"Is not Alonso do it."

The detective nodded in satisfaction. The woman was Alonso's mother or his woman. Who else would take the trouble to hide in his garden?

"Then who? Who did it?"

"There was a man staying at the hotel, name Fonseca, and a black man come see him in a white Toyota – dey call him Bullfrog. The two of dem kill him."

"How?"

There was a whispered conversation in the crotons. There are two of them out there, Swaby thought. He had a swig of beer and a rub of his belly and waited.

"They lick 'im on de head."

"Why?"

Silence and then, "Because de man has a plan to run to Canada wid de money."

"You saw dem do it?"

Silence except for a cricket.

"If you don't see it, how you know?"

"Because dey is drug-smuggling gangsters."

"How you know that?"

Another whispered conversation.

"Dat's for you to fin' out. You are de po-liceman. You expec' me to tell you all whilst you fin' out nuttin' and all you can do betwixt and between is arrest de wrong man."

"I know your voice," Swaby said. "You're the woman who came to the station and told me my mother was a leatherback turtle and my father was a blind lizard and I was a Aids-carrying battyman."

"No, I don't say dat," said Precious Ting.

"Goodnight," Swaby said.

***

Madame Juliette hustled Swaby through reception, across the patio, Gaugin-like with foliage, past the pool filled with white bodies, and into the office as quickly as the inspector could be hustled, encouraged or propelled. She did not like the police in the building; it lowered the tone. "This way, this way … a place cool enough to talk … How is your liver? And the children? This way, please."

Swaby was installed in the office, darkened by blinds, his back to the air-conditioning unit and a rum – a yes-as-it's-private-just-a-small-one – in his hand.

"If the newspaper forgets, everyone forgets," Madame Juliette offered.

"Sadly, not the police. Murder is murder. I must follow every clue, every rumour."

"Which are you following now?"

"Beg your pardon, Madame?"

"A clue or a rumour? And is it worth the trouble? Look at this from my point of view, Inspector. I have a hotel full of guests who know nothing about this old business of Chin Lee. I don't want one of them asking why there is a policeman in my office. Is something wrong?"

"The guests have changed but not the staff."

"The staff?"

"Your staff are the same and they keep talking."

"No problem for me. The guests do not understand a word they say."

"It would be better," the policeman said slowly, "if they said nothing at all."

"Ah. Who is talking?"

The policeman shrugged.

"I think I know. Am I right?"

"You say."

"Precious Ting."

Swaby nodded.

"What is she saying?"

"Never mind. Have you seen the watchman? Alonso?"

"No," said Madame Juliette firmly, relieved that she was able to answer the question truthfully. She had noticed irregularities in the kitchen and observed Precious Ting's new interest in walking on the beach but she had not seen Alonso. And strangely, she felt protective towards him as well; he was her employee and she guessed that he had been taken away as the scapegoat. If he had had the wit to escape, she did not want him recaptured or the whole nasty murder business reopened.

"Well, at least," the detective said, breathing deeply, reoxygenating to prepare for rising, "at least you can keep the staff from spreading rumours which may hamper police investigations. As you say, it makes bad business for both of us."

When Swaby had waddled his way across her patio and out of her life temporarily, Madame Juliette reflected on the purpose of his visit. The detective had asked only one question and that nothing to with the murder. However anxious he might be to solve the case, she could be forgiven for thinking he only wanted Precious Ting to shut up.

She went in search of the black diamond and found her, in a brief pause between duties, reading her Bible in the shade.

"Police say you pestering them."

"No, madame."

"Then what's this? A detective drive all the way from Negril Town to tell me nothing at all?"

"Is not Alonso kill de man."

"Who did it?"

"Nobody, madame."

"Nobody?"

"I don't know."

"You been talking around town?"

"No, madame."

"I'm warning you, Precious, if you make any trouble, if you bring the police here again, you're fired. You understand?"

"No, madame."

"The murder never happened. Do you understand?"

"If it never happen, madame, you can give Alonso back his job," Precious said, scoring a major point and making Madame Juliette pause.

"No, I can't do that. Go back to work."

Perversely, having sworn Precious to silence, Madame Juliette now wanted to know what she knew and where she'd got it from and how, and whether it was true. The desire to know fought the desire to play safe just briefly. For one mad moment, Madame Juliette did not care if her hotel burned in a blaze of scandal if she could only know who the villain was. Happily good sense returned before she could recall the maid.

***

At the upturned canoe, Alonso was catching hell.

"If I lose my job, 'cause of you, spider man, I kill you stone dead, stone dead."

Alonso was not perturbed. She had brought him some curried crab in the shell, bread and avocado pear. She obviously loved him and the murder threats were a sign of affection, a noise a woman made, a letting-off of steam.

Precious Ting boxed him on the side of the head, making his ears ring. "I will kill you stone dead, you hear me?"

Alonso waited for the ringing to subside, beating his head against his open palm. There was no doubt the woman was vexed, so he must reason with her. "But Precious, how you could lose your job?"

"You tell me to go see Swaby, tell him about dose two criminal. Swaby listen? No. Swaby come roun' dis morning to complain to Madame Juliette about me. You see anybody beggin' to give people a job in Jamaica? If you got one, you keep it, for if you lose it, you lose your name, your reputation. People say, 'Precious lose a good job, she mus' be t'ief or whore or some t'ing like dat!'"

"I suffer de same," Alonso said, dipping his finger in the curried crab. "Why you t'ink I is in such deep distress? I mus' repair my reputation and return to night watching which entail de 'ighest degree of trus'. Suspeck need not apply."

"An' de longes' hours for sleep, spider man."

She was becoming mollified, descending from boxing his ears to cheap shots about his personal habits.

"Spider man," he asked, "what is this spider man?"

"You look like one, meagre an' black an' long-legged. You are a Anansi man; you jinnal like him; you t'ief an' you lie an' you trickster."

Now she was flattering him so he put an arm round her shoulder and gave her a little hug. "I would look after you," he said.

She slapped his hand away, rose from the upturned canoe and stood in front of him, between him and the dazzling sea, her feet planted widely in the sand, arms akimbo, and she laughed. Alonso was mortified, he had not meant to be funny. He could not help admiring her at the same time, a little woman with all bits and pieces perfectly arranged, soft and strong, her head thrown back in laughter, a high aria of mockery. "What you laughin' at, Precious?"

"You can't look after puppy dog," she said. "You can't look after yourself. You can't get a job, you can't keep a job, you can't eat unless I feed you. You are worthless, Alonso, worthless!"

She was going too far. Loving a man was not bad, looking after him was better, but none of it was any good without respect. If a woman don't respect you, you must beat her and Precious was getting near to a beating. He decided to keep cool.

"Maybe so," he said, mildly, "maybe so, but I don't beat you," and as she drew breath to dare him to try, he added quickly, "and one thing is sure, you will not lose the job. You are the best in the hotel, the best-looking, the best-working, the best-natured. Madame J would be mad to dispense with you."

"I won't lose it if you leave. If you clear off, Alonso, just go away and leave me alone. Don't you has relations in Portland? Jus' go 'way, an' leave me in peace."

Alonso put the crab shells aside. "I can't do that," he said firmly. "I can run from Swaby, I can run from Ras and from Bullfrog, but I can't run from you because I does love you."

He looked up at her standing over him, favouring her with his most wistful, most little-boy-lost look. Precious wanted to laugh again and she wanted to cry, so she settled for a little smile. "Does love me, eh? Because I feed you."

"No," he said shaking his head, "no. I does love you because I do love you, an' that has no reason except yourself, your looks and your style an' all a dat. I does cherish you. I never talk to a woman like dis before, you know ... never."

He put a hand out to touch her hip and, leaning forward, slid it round her buttock, drawing her to him, and she took a step forward into the circle of his arms.

"You jus' want give me baby an' den you leave, like all Jamaica man. When belly swell, you gone."

The future being a long time away and not visible, Alonso refrained from perjuring himself. "A baby mother is a precious t'ing," he said.

"Well, not now," she replied, unhooking his hands from her backside. "It's broad daylight, people walkin' past, an' I has duties. I only come to tell you goodbye."

She sat down again beside him. She had started with this foolishness, he thought, and she was still saying it.

"All right, I'll go," he said, taking her hand and holding it. They sat together saying nothing, looking out to sea, savouring the anguish of parting, experiencing the pain of love which is the knowledge that it is transitory, that the ecstasy comes to nothing unless it be the creation of another entity who in time will suffer the same pain, the same futility.

"A baby mother is a precious t'ing."

"Not today, Alonso, not today."

"Tonight."

"No, sir."

"What am I going to do? Where you want me to go? You don't understan', Precious. I am between de devil an' de deep blue sea. If I go to Portland, I am still a murder suspeck! You can laugh but when policeman say 'Confess, boy!' you frighten. I don't care who or how many kill Chin Lee, and I don't care how, an' I don't care why dey do it. All I want is my job back an' to feel your body next to mine in de night. If people want to be drug smuggler, make money and construct Babylon, dat's okay. I just want my job back. Police don't want to solve de case so perhaps police in de drug business also."

Precious was too conservative to countenance such a suggestion. "No," she said firmly.

"Well, all right. Perhaps police 'fraid to get shot. I don't speak evil of any man, I just say 'perhaps'."

"Maybe so."

"Well, all right, if I can't get help from de police, where shall I turn? God is busy."

"Mr Bonanza."

"The Minister?"

"Yes. Magnus Bonanza."

This time it was Alonso's turn to laugh.

"Don't laugh. I telling you what the man said. The man said, 'Drug smugglers, hang the brutes.' That's what the Minister said to me, to me personal and to the American millionaire, right there in the bar of the Casuarina. 'We must stamp out the drug trade!' That's what he said."

"The Minister is a high and mighty man. How I going to reach him?"

"Das for you to contrive."

"I has no money an' de police looking for me. You want me to get a taxi-cab and go to Kingston to call on government?"

10

The said Bonanza, a rum in one hand and a pâté-smothered biscuit in the other, was reclining on a cushion in the cockpit of *Swingtime* as the yacht approached Kingston harbour. The treacherous waters of the 'sand hills' were smoothed for the ministerial passage. *Swingtime* glided through a coppery sea, its surface broken only by the occasional flying fish eluding barracuda. The ginger man was coiling ropes, the upright alligator inhaling nicotine, the hairy engineer consulting charts, and Leprosini, at the wheel, oiling himself to make his pectorals glisten. Carlotta, to be as far away from him as possible, was perched in the pulpit, the lovely legs dangling toward the water, watching the landfall.

The old fortifications and brick barracks of Port Royal were quite close, low on the horizon, palms rising among them, and various rusty wrecks and fishing vessels sheltered in the lee of the old town. Small boys splashed and shouted and chased each other on the grey beach.

Beyond, across the silver sheet of the harbour, was Kingston. The chimney of the cement factory at Harbour Head sent a great plume of smoke against Long Mountain. So the city, except for the new skyscrapers on the water front, was obscured by a blanket of smog, competing for squalor and ill health with cities larger and more famous.

Channel markers, weed-grown traffic lights inhabited by pelicans, guided *Swingtime* through the small-boat channel close to the mangroves. A jumbo jet painted red and yellow thundered overhead, lowering her wheels for landing, and a Taiwanese freighter was stationary off number two pier, without crew, apparently abandoned. *Swingtime* sought the backwater among the mangroves converted into a marina by the still Royal Jamaica Yacht Club, filled with sailboats, motor sailers, powerboats and noisy gulls. Above the marina, the shingled two-storey clubhouse beckoned, with its freshwater pool, its open-sided bar and marlin mounted over the ping-pong table.

Bonanza's limousine was waiting under the almond trees, its chauffeur asleep with his feet through the window. The Minister debarked and made the briefest of farewells, for landing took away the comfort of the sea. Stepping ashore was stepping into hell, for the soil burned and the atmosphere was a fan-assisted oven. The air-conditioned trip to town awaited and, politeness over, Bonanza fled. Fonseca followed him, begging a lift. The ginger man and the engineer, breaking sweat, busied themselves with fuel and supplies, Carlotta with checking victuals, but Leprosini would not leave her to it, summoning her to the clubhouse bar to watch him drink his Perrier.

"My flight goes in an hour. Come with me. Those guys can sail her to Florida and they know what to do."

"They'll need a cook."

"Are you kidding?"

"I prefer to stay with them."

"You don't like me, do you?"

"I hate you."

"You sound like my wife. Okay, sweetheart, get your arse off my boat and find your own way back to England." Leprosini rose, shouted to the barman to get him a cab and went back to the yacht to get his sea-bag and his briefcase. Carlotta noticed that the barman, reading his paper, had paid no attention to Leprosini's request. Obviously he had, for some obscure Jamaican reason, been offended and was preparing to do nothing. Anything that would frustrate the great man would entertain Carlotta, but she wanted him off the island, and by dint of a few sirs and a few smiles she got the barman to telephone the airport taxi service and, a job well done, ordered herself a rum punch and arranged for the ice on the yacht to be replenished.

***

The euphoria occasioned by seeing the back of Leprosini was quickly replaced by the threat of nostalgia. Looking at the sweet lines of *Swingtime,* Carlotta remembered that she had been dismissed and sentenced to return to England. Thinking of going, she began to miss what she had taken for granted. The ginger man was coming towards the verandah bar, drifting across in the glare. He approached slowly enough for her to study him, something she realised that, concentrating on her aversion to his skipper, she had not done.

His name was Stephen and he was wearing a white sun hat, so he had no face. She could fill that in: blue eyes, a shortish nose and a wide mouth – the sort they call generous – a cheerful peasant face hanging between bright red ears, speckled with ginger stubble. His shoulders were broad and as muscled as they were freckled, the muscles not etched but padded, suggesting that he might, in later years, look like a beer barrel. His shorts were dirty, and the yachtsman's knife and spike hung from his belt like a six-gun. The hair on his legs was burned silver by the sun. The crepe soles of his topsiders protected him, walking on coals.

The ginger man, Stephen, suddenly real, pulled out the chair opposite her, and settled, leaning back, legs sprawled. "Where's the boss?"

"Gone."

"Already?"

There was the sound over the palisadoes of giant jet engines threatening take-off.

"That'll be him. He said you guys could sail her to Florida and you knew what to do. Probably he doesn't want to be on board if you run into the baddies."

Stephen's blue eyes were as wide and innocent as the heavens. He tossed the sun hat on the table, revealing a pink pressure band on the skin of his forehead, and called over his shoulder to the barman for a Stripe. "Maybe the boss has better things to do. Big business and such."

"He's fired me."

"Oh yeah. What do you mean?"

Carlotta, playing with it, snapped the plastic swizzle stick that had decorated her rum punch. " 'Fired' means told me I'm out of a job; I get off his boat and go home."

Stephen gave that a lot of thought. "Do you want to do that?" he asked.

"Do I have a choice?"

"Sure, everybody has a choice."

"I didn't … how shall I say … live up to his expectations."

"I can't imagine that," the ginger man said, innocence appraising loveliness, "there must be something wrong with him. But you still have a choice."

"It's his boat."

"Sure. But he could change his mind."

"Why?"

"Come on, Carlotta, think. By blackmail. Knowing what you must know by now, if you want in, you're in."

The barman arrived with an ice-cold Stripe and Stephen gave him two dollars, *you-ess*, muttering that he could keep the change. Carlotta was contemplating the broken swizzle stick. She could defy Leprosini and stay on the boat. She'd need some sort of back-up mechanism like the phone number of an honest policeman, but she had visited no cemeteries recently. It was okay for the ginger man to encourage her, but what would Leprosini do about it? He surely wouldn't accept the flouting of his authority.

"Who's going to protect me?"

"Three guesses."

Here we go again, Carlotta thought. It's a man's world; you get what you want, but you pay for it in sexual currency. It would be more than daft to exchange a rich man for a poor one, even if the poor man was a warm sensitive human being with a bigger ...

"I'm gay," Stephen said. "You don't have to worry about me, but I would look after you."

"What about Selwyn?"

"He's gay too. The boss only likes gay guys on board, then there's no competition."

"Is that the reason?" Carlotta said, thinking there might be another. "Are you and Selwyn an item?"

"No," Stephen said. "He gives me the creeps."

"I think I need another of these."

"Swizzle sticks?"

"Rum punch."

They sat in silence while it was made and served. The world had flipped like a pancake in a skillet two or three times in the last half hour, and Carlotta needed to regroup. "Tell me about Fonseca."

"He's not queer."

"I didn't mean that."

"He's just a house lizard."

"A snapper-up of flies."

"Right."

"And Bullfrog?"

"The ugly one? He's a general."

"A general?"

"Kills people for a living. You want to know about Chin Lee?"

Carlotta looked out over the masts in the marina across the harbour to the smoke-smudge of Kingston, and the Blue Mountains blurred in cloud. "No, I don't," she said. "Maybe he knew too much, maybe he thought he could do what he liked."

"Something like that," Stephen agreed. "Are you leaving or staying?"

***

Alonso set out for Kingston, walking. He had no money and no hope, but he had a purpose, impossible as it might seem: to see Magnus Bonanza, to restore his reputation, regain his job and remain adjacent to Precious Ting. He had only gone a few miles when it occurred to him that this walking business was overrated. He was going to ruin his shoes. So he sat down, took them off, tied the shoelaces together and hung them round his neck. He made some distance before the sun on the asphalt made it too hot and sticky for walking, so he sat down on a milestone and rested.

A man with a donkey-cart helped him out for a mile or so. Then he boarded a country bus which got him to some place that looked like a village, where he was ejected for non-possession of fare. On the cliff-top nearby was a sign saying 'Lookout Bar', a hut in a circle of whitewashed stones, with one so-so table with a thatched umbrella which was clearly the reason for the name. There were two white people, man and woman, looking out and sipping bottled fruit juice. Their little car, a Ford Fiesta, was heating in the sun. The couple seemed totally entranced by each other and by the bit of blue sea running below them, though as far as Alonso could see there was nothing special about them or that part of the ocean. The car was untended.

Alonso doubled over like a commando, scooted behind the vehicle and knelt by the rear tyre. Unscrewing the valve cap he pressed the little nipple with the end of a stick. To cover the hiss of escaping air, Alonso made faraway animal noises: the bawling of a calf for its mother, a donkey braying and the hysterical yapping of a dog drawing attention to itself. Neither the hiss nor the animal imitations turned the heads of the tourists and, with a final sigh, the tyre settled on the rim, the rubber spread and flattened.

Alonso perched on a whitewashed stone and waited. He was so still the couple did not notice him as they approached. The man had courteously installed the woman and was circling the car when Alonso called out, "Hey, mister man, you got a flat tyre."

"Shit," said the man.

"You got a pump?" Alonso asked.

"I don't think so. It's a hired car. I don't know."

"Let us see," Alonso said, taking charge, and coming confidently forward. He opened the boot, removed the tourists' luggage and rooted around inside. "No, no pump, but you has a spare and a jack. This what you call a tyre tool. Stand back. I tell you what, mister, you and the lady go have another drink and I'll fix it for you."

"He's going to want money," the woman whispered.

"That's okay with me," the man said.

"Make a deal before he does it. He could take you for a ride."

"Not with a flat tyre, honey," the man joked.

"No money," Alonso said, inserting the jack. "I don't want money. Welcome to Jamaica."

Totally bemused, the couple stayed to watch. Their cameras were around their necks, their money in their wallets, but could they trust this seemingly amiable fellow with their suitcases and their car? Alonso, as he worked, explained his expertise by telling them he had lost his job in a garage, times being hard, and was on his way to find another. However hard life was, he philosophised, one should find time to help one's neighbour. That, he said, was how the poor survived, by helping each other, and that is why they would inherit the kingdom. Only the rich, he said, could be independent, but independence made them lonely and selfish, through no fault of their own, he added, tightening the nuts. "How far you going?" Alonso asked.

"We're going round the island."

"Nice, nice, you'll have a lovely time. It's a beautiful island. Everybody say so." He put the tools away, replaced the suitcases, and opened the door for the woman, shutting it discreetly like a practised doorman.

The man was clearly embarrassed. "I'd like to do something for you," he said, hand moving towards his wallet.

"No, no, no obligation, sir!"

"I'd like to do something."

"All right," Alonso said, getting into the back seat, "you can drop me off in Kingston."

***

Kingston is ideal for a wanted man. Alonso felt like a raindrop fallen in the sea. In twenty square miles of poverty, who would notice him, talk about him, or arrest him? On the other hand, who would feed him? That as usual was the big snag. To be a grass louse on the biggest cow in the world was no good without a purchase, a place to bite, your own taste of the blood of the host.

He went down to Coronation Market to use his charm on the market woman. Alonso was a specialist on the internal bruising of vegetables and fruit and the identification of unsaleable goods, so he was able to collect enough to barter for a couple of fish heads and some salt. Around the corner, he found a woman with an empty pot who offered to cook his soup for him. Her thin-legged children appeared from somewhere, attracted by the smell, and in a stroke Alonso acquired a family. But generous as he was, when he doled out the soup he made sure he had the best of it, for, he reminded himself, if he was to be a breadwinner for this collection of skeletons, he had to keep up his strength.

***

The Ministry, a concrete rectangle riddled with windows, overlooked a dusty park – a public space too trodden for grass, where thousands of children played, cricket balls ran through the football fields, paths intersected everywhere, dogs cringed out of the way of missiles, and little tornadoes of dust rose and whirled away in the heat haze. The building itself, once modern, was a monument to the deficiencies of its builder and architect. It was ugly. Weather stains streaked the walls, the windows no longer fitted, the air-conditioning no longer worked, the corridors were gloomy, the water fountains dry, but in the box-like offices young black men in white shirt-sleeves and tight-bodiced girls smelling of sweat and perfume still did the business of the nation, moving dog-eared piles of paper from one desk to another.

Somewhere on the top floor, reached by the last functioning lift, was the sanctum of Magnus Bonanza. His air-conditioning did work, his clean windows overlooked the poinciana in bloom, his floor was carpeted like the offices of ministers in temperate lands, a six-by-eight-foot blown-up photograph of a bauxite plant graced one wall, and another of similar size, an aerial shot of the Casuarina Hotel and Negril Beach, hung on the other. His mahogany desk had an alabaster penholder, a tooled leather blotting pad, four telephones and a framed photograph of Mrs Bonanza and the boys. The Jamaican flag rested on a liquor cabinet with built-in ice-maker, a present from Leprosini, and in a small, littered, adjacent cubicle lived Miss Pearl, the big brown lady who ran the Ministry.

Alonso was not such a fool as to think he could just walk in and say "Mawnin'". There was a policeman outside the main entrance and a glimpse of uniforms in the lobby but there were no guards in the parking lot by the sign that said 'Minister', so Alonso decided to loiter in that vicinity. He was not alone. Various supplicants in positions of studied nonchalance had had the same idea, and when the limousine appeared it was instantly, though respectfully, surrounded by citizens muttering about "rice", or "saltfish", or "import licence", or "loan", or "hunger", to all of which, as he was escorted by chauffeur and plainclothes man, the minister replied, "Not today."

The phrase carried, if not a promise, at least an implication that they might be heard tomorrow and something might some other day be done. One impetuous and dissatisfied old hag shattered the decorum of the Minister's passage with a loud scream, "If I vote for you again, Magnus, God strike me dead!"

This was greeted, as tragedy is among the tragic, by hilarious laughter.

Alonso, briefly near the Minister, loud-whispered, "Chin Lee."

The Minister did not hear, or appeared not to hear him, and smiling, waving and repeating "not today", took cover indoors.

Alonso went for a stroll in the park to plan his next move. One of the men in the parking lot had used an interesting phrase, "import licence". Madame Juliette back at the hotel was always complaining about them, or the lack of them, and they seemed somehow necessary to life. He would get one, post haste.

Bravely Alonso entered the Ministry, ignoring the uniforms that ignored him, an unarmed countryman of no consequence. He got into the crowd milling around the reception desk and elbowed his way to the front, trying to catch the eye of a grey-haired man who it seemed had been hired for his ability to look the other way.

"Import licence," Alonso said.

"First floor," the man said.

Alonso climbed the concrete steps, entering the throat of the monster lit by glass bricks above the landing, littered by cigarette butts, candy wrappers and flecks of paint that had peeled off the metal hand rails. The stairs released him into a hot dim corridor down which a woman was pushing a trolley with bottled drinks and sugared doughnuts.

"Import licence?" he asked. She only half-turned to point at a door with a glass panel but a doughnut was already off the tray, in the hand and behind the back. It was eaten before he reached the door and pushed it open to enter another waiting area with another blind receptionist. Approaching, he was halted by a fellow-patient who pointed at a bench, already occupied. "You're last," he said.

An hour later, belly rumbling again, knees weak and mouth dry, Alonso had his turn. "Import licence."

"For what?"

"Apple."

"That's agricultural. Next floor."

"I have to see Minister. De man say I mus' see Minister personally."

"Which man?"

"Boss man." He had to think of a really impressive name. "Boss man, Mr Stockhausen."

"Do you have an appointment?"

"But of course," Alonso said, expansively.

"Why you come in here?"

"Somebody sen' me."

129

"Top floor," she said.

Alonso made his way out, hoping the doughnut lady was still in sight, but she had disappeared. The steps seemed steeper than before but they eventually ran out, leaving him in another grey corridor where, at the far end, a man sat on a stool, guarding a slightly larger door. Alonso assumed his most aristocratic manner, walking briskly with his head thrown back and his toes turned out until he drew alongside. "I have an appointment with the Minister."

"What's your name?"

"Chin Lee."

"Das a Chinyman name."

"Not your business how I name."

"You look like a damn nigger man to me."

"Jus' announce me, please," Alonso said haughtily.

The man rose and went through the door, releasing a cool draught of conditioned air into the fetid corridor, and closed it carefully behind him. Alonso waited. Five minutes was all he needed, five minutes to sort the whole thing out, to get help from the top, from a man who mattered. Five minutes he waited, and then the khaki uniform returned, filled with the triumph of brief authority.

"Miss Pearl say you have no appointment. She will not bother the Minister. You mus' get out de building in two shakes or de police will be alerted."

***

Alonso traced the Minister to his home in Jacks Hill, a modest bungalow in the swimming-pool-and-Alsatian-dog belt, which overlooked the tilted plain of Kingston, grey-green by day, spangled with neon by night.

Reconnoitring the place while the Minister was away sacrificing himself for the community, Alonso attempted to make friends with the dog. Stinking of fear, he allowed the

130

animal to sniff at his trouser leg through the grillwork of the gate, but this enraged the beast to an ecstasy of growling, snarling and teeth baring. Alonso had no food to offer it, lacking any himself. He tried chatting to it through the bars in a wheedling tone, like a mother charming her baby through the slats of a crib. This made the dog withdraw, but only halfway up the short drive, giving itself room and momentum for a charge. With a bloodcurdling howl it leapt at Alonso, crashed into the gate, all but stunning itself, and set off burglar alarms all over the house.

Alonso stood his ground, for to run from a dog is suicide. Innocence, he thought, is the best defence except in law, where it means nothing. The burglar alarms brought somebody out of the house, a thin spidery-looking old maid with stockings rolled down to her ankles, wearing a blue uniform topped by a pink angora cardigan. Her greying hair was done in a pattern of pigtails like a girl's, and she walked with one hand on her hip. "Move off!" she said, waving the other hand. "Move off, or I let out de dawg and sick 'im 'pon you!"

"No, missis," said Alonso stoutly, "you can't do dat."

"You loiterin'. Move off!"

"No, ma'am. I is here wid purpose."

"What you want?"

"I has to see Minister."

"Den go down to de Ministry. Down dere so!" she shrieked, pointing in the direction of the city.

"I do dat a'ready."

"Move off, bwoy!"

Alonso smiled. "You're a nice-looking lady. I see you has an understanding face," he improvised, in spite of the evidence. "I walk all de way from Negril to see de Minister."

"You could walk from hell, just walk back. Come dawg." With the Alsatian in tow, she started back towards the house.

"Excuse me," Alonso called. "You are the Minister's mother?"

"What?"

"You are Minister mother?"

The old hag laughed, showing a gold tooth. At least her amusement was delaying her departure. "His mother dead."

"Auntie?"

"I am his housekeeper."

"How do you do, ma'am," oozed Alonso. "My name is Alonso Patterson."

"Move off."

"The Minister must rely greatly on you. More so than on that Miss Pearl at the Ministry. Housekeeping is the important thing. Life is what you eat and where you sleep, the rest is passing time. Yes, you are the kingpin!"

"Patterson?" she said, interested in a man so understanding.

"Yes. You know the West Indies fast bowler? Is my cousin," Alonso lied smoothly. "And you name, missis?"

"Foster. Mary Lou Foster."

"I don't know any Foster except one, a fellow name Romeo, work in de coas'guard."

"My nephew!"

"Would you believe it!"

So it was that Alonso, in return for clearing the leaves from the pool – the yard boy had gone to the doctor with a sore foot – found himself in the Minister's kitchen, the Alsatian at his feet and a plate on his lap – roast pork, crackling, and rice and peas saturated in gravy – listening to Mary Lou detail her aches and pains, and express her faith in Jesus who had brought her through so many trials and tribulations to the very gates of Paradise, and who was waiting to dip her in the healing stream, put a crown on her head and give her a place in the angelic choir. After that, Alonso had a nap, his head on a pile of Mrs Bonanza's underwear beside the Westinghouse in the laundry room.

***

Mrs Bonanza was playing bridge and the boys had gone to a party at the Matalon house, so Magnus had the twinkling city to himself, alone with a bottle of Appleton Gold and his dreams for Jamaica's future.

"Excuse me, Mr Magnus, a man come to see you," said Mary Lou from the doorway to the living room. The light behind her made her look like a stick woman, a stick woman witch, Bonanza thought, and under her broom there was a scrawny fellow with country written all over him, worse than country – bush. But Bonanza did not protest. If Mary Lou had vetted the individual he could have five minutes; not a seat, or a drink, but five minutes. He raised a hand, waggled two beckoning fingers, and Alonso came out on to the terrace.

"Come round, so I can see you," Bonanza said, not moving, and Alonso advanced into the light.

"Alonso Patterson, sir,"

"So what can I do for you?"

"I am night watchman at the Casuarina Hotel ..."

Bonanza did his imitation of Buddha, his belly bulging out of his shirt and an enigmatic smile frozen on his face. "I was there the night the Chinyman got killed ..."

"But you're the boy dat kill him," the Minister said, pointing the finger.

"No, sah, is not me do it but dey lock me up, an' I fight against injustice, like you, Minister. I escape an' hide in de bush wid de Army of Jah, which is nuttin' but a cavalcade of rascals. So I run from dem, an' a hairplane lan' on m' head whilst I was sleepin' in a culvert. It come from Columbia wid a cargo of cocaine, an' I know what boat dat same cocaine

133

leavin' Jamaica on, an' I know who kill Chin Lee, an' so I come to see you."

"Maybe you know too much."

"Yes, sir. But is not me do it, an' I need you to help me, sir."

"What's your name again?" Bonanza, his brain slowed by alcohol, needed time.

"Alonso."

"Yes. Why you come to see me?"

Alonso was patient. "Because it is not me do it, is not me kill de Chinyman, and you is a fighter for justice and a righter of wrong."

"Ah," said the Minister. Perhaps the fellow had made no connection between himself and the others, or perhaps he was smarter than he looked and this was an opening pitch for blackmail. "Sit down, Alonso."

Alonso perched. Bonanza poured himself another rum and contemplated the starry heavens. If it were blackmail, he wouldn't pay, he would resign. Jamaica, thank God, was still a democracy, so you could make your pile and get out without being shot or even going to jail. This could be the end and, glass in hand, he was almost resigned to it. Chin Lee or not, he would probably lose in the next election. Voters like a bit of corruption, it makes you human and gives them something to gossip about. Then suddenly, for no reason, they turn against you. Maybe it was time to go, he had made almost enough. Almost. The bungalow at Negril would be finished soon, there was money in Switzerland to let Mrs Bonanza loose in Paris once a year, money in Florida to educate the boys, and a little bit in a bank in Grand Cayman for unspecified expenditures. Almost enough, almost enough.

The man was still sitting there.

"So how can I help you, Alonso?" Bonanza repeated.

"I know you has a good reputation, sir, and I hear you is against the drug business. Precious heard you speaking on the matter in the bar. 'Hang the brutes,' you said, 'Mow them down.' Quite right, sir."

This harping on drugs settled it in the Minister's mind. The intruder was no innocent and this was blackmail. Bonanza's reputation was swept away by anger. He wanted to get up and smash the bottle over the little bastard's head, and cut his throat with the broken bit. But Mary Lou was hovering in the living room, and his own conviction for assault, or murder, would not help.

"Yes, indeed," Bonanza said, sounding like an old seventy-eight, "the drug trade is the scourge of Jamaica and we must do everything we can to stop it."

"They deserve to hang, that's so."

The waters of Bonanza's life whirled down the drain. "What do you want?" he pleaded.

"Help, sir."

"How much help?"

"I want you tell de police. Tell dem is not me do it. Tell dem is Fonseca an' Bullfrog, an' tell dem where de drugs is gone ..."

Bonanza raised a hand like a traffic policeman. "One small detail, boy, can you prove any of this?"

"Prove? I jus' talkin' but I know what I talkin' 'bout. I can't prove, but I can talk. I can tell everybody everyt'ing. You understan', sir, I don't wish to remain a wanted man, a murder suspeck. An' I want compensation."

Why didn't the bugger state his terms, name a figure? He'd asked him a thousand times. "How much?"

"Plenty," Alonso said, airily. "An' I wants my job back."

"Your job?"

"Watchie. Das de mos' important. I wants trust an' I wants my good name."

Bonanza sighed. "I think we can come to some arrangement. Leave it with me, Alonso. You just keep quiet for a while, lie low, and I'll work on it behind the scenes." His hand went into his pocket.

"Here, here is a little something to be going on with."

Alonso looked at the money in his hand. He hadn't expected that. What a generous man this Minister was! Generous.

"You going back to Negril?"

"No, sir."

"Where are you staying?"

"I don't know de name of de place, sir."

"What district?"

"Out near de race track, sir. Dere's a scrap iron yard, an' a billboard wid a brown gal wid a big smile an' a bottle of Three Dagger. There are various of the poor livin' as best they can."

"I don't pass that way often, so I won't try to find you," Bonanza said. "You come back and see me next week, eh? We'll see what can be done about you in the meantime."

Alonso started back into the house but Bonanza pointed him towards the gate.

"I jus' want to say goodnight to Miss Foster," Alonso explained, "and thank her for the feed."

Bonanza couldn't be bothered to reply. The fool was welcome to the meal and the civilities. He might not have many more of them.

The Minister did some slow, careful thinking. He heard the muttered valedictions from the kitchen, the clanging of the driveway gate, and followed Alonso's progress down Jacks Hill by identifying the voices of his neighbours' dogs, each in turn speeding the visitor's departure. Then he heaved himself out of his chair, the smooth tiles cold on his bare feet, and went indoors to his study, picked up the phone and dialled a number he knew by heart.

"A man was here," Bonanza said, "has proof you killed Chin Lee … You listening?"

"What's de name?" said a soft bass voice.

"Alonso Patterson."

"I know. He got away from me before. Where is he?"

Bonanza told him all he knew. The bass voice muttered something about not being paid for the last job yet, and Bonanza said, "If you want *you-ess*, you have to wait."

***

When the first shot was fired, Alonso thought an election campaign had started. At the second, a revolution. Only at the third did he realise somebody was shooting at him. A bullet hit the zinc fence behind his head with a sound that made his ears ring. Alonso sprinted, hurdled the cactus hedge at the bottom of the yard and ran on, not thinking where. Somebody shouted, "Go, bwoy, go!" and somebody else shouted, "Stop t'ief!" A woman shrieked with laughter, and chickens ran this way and that, squawking as chickens do without knowing why.

Then he saw the Toyota coming down the lane, a lane not used to motor vehicles, knocking over washtubs and cardboard boxes and baskets, and running right over a baby lying in the dirt without killing it, without even touching it.

Alonso changed course, zigzagged through another dusty yard, shacks built around a lignum vitae tree, scaled another fence and slid down the concrete and stone embankment of a giant drainage ditch built to carry flood water and the refuse of the city into the harbour. As it was the dry season, the ditch was floored with pebbles, empty tins, scraps of plastic and low scrub. Alonso went to ground and lay still, blowing hard.

In the instant he had recognised the van, the thin brown man at the wheel and the thick black man beside him. They had followed him, and Kingston was no longer a safe haven. Instead of being anonymous, obscured by numbers in the big city, he was marked simply by being a stranger. He couldn't afford to wait a week for his friend Mr Bonanza to help him. He didn't want the charges dropped after he was dead.

But what to do? And where to go? While the sun was up, nowhere. Which suited him, as all that running wasn't really his style. Lying there with one ear in the dirt but his eyes open, contemplating a mound of rubbish, he saw a scorpion emerging from a corned beef tin. The lethal little beast was due to pass only ten inches from his nose. Alonso did not move but his hand closed on a stone, a weapon just in case. "Don't trouble me, scorpy," he whispered, "and I don't trouble you."

The scorpion sailed away, his tail curled over his back like a flag of truce. Alonso watched as he disappeared down a dusty hole, his size and colour.

"Each to his own home," Alonso said, "and mine is bush."

When night came, he rose and set off down the drain in the moonlight.

11

Three days of wind funnelled between Cuba and Hispaniola had set great billows rolling toward the eastern point of Jamaica, and though the wind had died the waves kept up their monstrous heaving. Against them, rounding the point, *Swingtime* made slow progress. Though steadied by her cargo of cocaine stuffed into carved and painted parrots, wrapped in sacking and neatly stored in packing cases, *Swingtime* pitched horribly. For comfort's sake, Stephen kept her throttled down, but it was still a roller-coaster passage, the bow sliding down into a trough, seeming as if it would never rise again and that the next wave would wash over them, then, creaking and groaning, she would start to climb, pointing at the leaden sky, her stern almost awash. From the top of each wave there was a magnificent view of Jamaica, of a black canoe balanced on another wave, and the top of someone else's mast, then, in a trough a view of nothing but the wave rising ominously in front and hurrying away behind, leaving streaks of foam and sea-weed.

Past the candy-striped lighthouse they headed northwest, then west to cruise between Cuba and Jamaica. On this stretch, the weather calmed, the breeze astern was balmy, Stephen put up sail and, motor-assisted, they scooted along the North Coast and south of the Gardens of the Queen, headed for a rendezvous, a certain point along a certain stretch of shallow muddied water, somewhere off a mangrove swamp, somewhere near an unnamed fishing port on the Gulf Coast of Florida, a rendezvous with fortune.

Sufficient unto the day were the evils and the profits thereof. In the long limbo of the voyage, they relaxed.

Carlotta produced cold beer and potato crisps packaged like tennis balls, Stephen set the boat on automatic pilot, and under the awning Selwyn took off his musical T-shirt to show the black rug on his chest and little pink nipples like rosebuds in a forest. "Where's Leprosini now, I wonder?"

Stephen looked at his watch. "I know exactly where he is. Cannes. Cannes, France – in case there's one in Louisiana."

"He goes?"

"He goes."

"What for? Does he make films as well as build hotels?"

"He buys and sells porn."

"Why did I ask? But it's too downmarket for him."

"He's at the top end of the down market, if you follow me. He has a small line in out-takes, videos of out-takes, like Shirley Temple with some black guy, John Wayne being mutilated by Indians, or Ronald Reagan as a Greek shepherd."

"You're making it up," Carlotta said firmly.

Stephen lay on his back for the longest time, staring at the awning, and then said, "I hope so. But how can I be sure? There'd be money in any of those."

Selwyn giggled, encouraging him.

"You see, Carlotta, he doesn't deal in ordinary hard stuff like 'The Nun and The Gardener' or 'Whips, Handcuffs and Iron Bars', he has a line in stuff he sells exclusively to Arab princes. The idea is that each video is unique, a one-off, like a Rembrandt or something, no copies, so when they have a showing in the movie tent, none of the other sheikhs have ever seen it before, things like the ritual murder of little boys …"

"That's enough, Stephen," Carlotta said.

But Stephen was in full flow. "He's working on a version of *The Golden Ass*. He's got a donkey but he's still looking for the girl …"

"Shut up, Stephen," Carlotta said. "Just shut up! To think I was beginning to like you."

"That's the way it is," Selwyn sighed.

"What I'm trying to tell you," Stephen said, rising on an elbow to look at her, "is that I hate the man. He is Satan himself."

"Then why do you work for him?"

"'Aha!' he cried, and pointed at her," Stephen said, doing just that. "Pots and kettles. You were fired; why did you stay?"

"I had nothing else to do."

"Not good enough," said the other devil, pushing back the tangled locks. "If you are doing Evil, the Good must be clearly in sight. The End must justify the Means. I am engineer on this boat because it has a wonderful engine that needs no looking after. So I have all the time I need to study, to master the techniques of corporate fraud and insider trading. Such crime is best because it inspires admiration not revenge. You rob millions of little fish, but no one of them has reason enough to kill you, and the other big fish are all doing the same thing so they merely congratulate you."

"You'll never get a chance to get near that stuff."

"Why not? Because I'm a dirty little gay with long hair and bow legs? Just wait. That will be the last stage of my preparation – a haircut, a grey flannel suit, a frame house in Connecticut ..."

"You'll need a wife, kids and a station wagon."

"They can be got cheap. Second-hand."

"And you, Stephen?"

"I like sailing. I'd like to settle somewhere that's not San Francisco. Sea Island, Georgia, maybe, or the Bahamas. Do we own the Bahamas? No. Doesn't matter. Some place like that. Tar-paper sleeping shacks and a big kitchen and dining hut down by the shore. I'd have a sort of permanent summer camp for kids, teach them to swim and sail and fish, and do green things, you know, like taking care of the sea, the reefs and the coral. But I don't want kids who can pay! I don't want parents who can buy that experience, who can give their privileged little legitimates something to remember when they rejoin the rat race. I want it to be the place. I want it to be the last place. I want kids fresh out of prison, kids who've been tortured and beaten and starving in slums, kids who are dying of Aids. I don't want them to come and go. I want them to stay. We'd work out a way of living from the sea, without selling anything, without hurting it, or anybody."

"What about you, Carlotta?" Selwyn said. "That you've got nothing better to do isn't good enough. We've played the truth game, told you our dreams and our ambitions. I'm going to make a fortune out of false accounting and Stephen's going to be a good guy, running a nautical ashram in some country where he won't be arrested for child abuse. What about you? What do you want to be doing when the first worry line appears, the first extra ounce on the haunch, the first time you think about a face lift?"

Carlotta looked out at the blue waves, hurrying to keep up, letting her mind rest in their movement and their colour. "If I knew," she said sweetly, "I'd probably be doing it now."

***

Precisely on time and at the appointed place – a bit of grey sea-water selected by the automatic navigation system, accurate to twenty yards anywhere in the world, perfected by the US Air Force and manufactured in Japan – *Swingtime* cut her engine and drifted. It was the hour before dawn and a light mist hung on the face of the deep. The deck was damp with dew, making Carlotta's thighs cold as she sat on the stern rail. Stephen and Selwyn manhandled four large black poly-styrene tubs up from below and over the side. The tubs had been made in Poland for shipping strawberry pulp to jam factories, and they were light, waterproof and cheap. They fell in the water with a comforting plop, bobbed and bumped a couple of times and floated gently away into the dawn.

Carlotta revved the engine, the bow swung westward and they chugged away, innocent and free. Stephen put the deep-sea rod in the socket while Selwyn rummaged in the tackle box. Carlotta left the wheel on automatic and went below to make coffee. When the coastguard helicopter flew over them at first light they waved cheerfully, three college kids in Daddy's boat out looking for marlin, or love.

The helicopter in turn signalled to the police launch which, assisted by bleeps from the strawberry tubs, made a beeline for them, swung them onboard with a life-saving lift, and headed for a creek in the mangroves. Up this, at Captain Ted's Lobster Landing, the tubs – four tiny elephants without legs – were rolled along the jetty and into the back of a truck of which the cab, discreetly lettered, read 'Continental, Interstate and Alaskan', the initial letters of each word bold in red, white and blue.

Two days later the strawberry tubs were opened in the stock room of a store in a shopping plaza in Francistown, New Jersey; an establishment called 'Bolivar's Boutique' which sold South American curios, bark paintings, pottery, hand-woven rugs, salad bowls and primitive sculpture. It was run by a man named Morris, who was no relation to Leprosini. Only one parrot was displayed at a time, but they proved popular. They were bought by a police sergeant, a schoolteacher, a play-ground superintendent, a male nurse and a man in a black Mercedes, among others. They all paid cash.

***

Big Man travelled only at night when the narrow Jamaican roads were free of flatfooted, big-bottomed women with trays or baskets on their heads, of donkeys with hampers like wings, pigs, goats and small children riding handcarts, one foot on and the other foot pushing, or tourists in air-conditioned cars, or herds of cattle being moved from one dry pasture to another. He travelled at night to keep his tyres cool, and because he liked nothing better than sleeping in the day.

Alonso had made himself a nest in the back of Big Man's truck. With his feet propped up against the tailgate, his back supported by bags of chicken feed and his arms by cases of beer, he could relax and contemplate the starry heavens. The stars, however, bounced around too much, so he closed his eyes and dozed. He was on his way back to the west end, to Negril, and every swerve and exaggerated gear change was taking him further away from those murderers and closer to Precious Ting. Through Spanish Town, Old Harbour, May Pen and Mandeville in the warm scented night, oh, it was good to be alive a little longer!

Bluefields is no more than two shacks and a Coca Cola sign, but the main South Coast road does pass through it, filling the narrow strip between the mountains and the sea. In the swamp where the white egrets nest, the road becomes a booby trap. It makes a sharp left turn, in front of which a bump tilts the headlights to the mountainside so the road itself is invisible. To make things worse, the left turn has subsided toward the swamp so the camber goes the wrong way. Though he had negotiated it many times before, Big Man in his cab, having recalled some past sexual glory, had lost his concentration. The truck slid, toppled and crashed, throwing the chicken feed into the swamp and Alonso into the mangroves. The branches received him gently, as if he too had come to roost.

Romeo Foster, in bed when he heard the crash, was accustomed to passing trucks, able to sleep through them, but the screech, the crash, the silence woke him. His wife, now so far advanced in pregnancy she had been banished to the floor, was also instantly awake, tapping at him. "Romeo, vehicle mash up in de swamp" she said. "You better go see if anybody dead."

***

Alonso was taking his time. Looking down, he saw Big Man climb out of the cab and pull his sideman out after him. They were cursing so loud and swearing so much that he knew they were unhurt. He could forget about them, as they had no doubt forgotten about him. Cradled by mangrove, he ran a body check: both legs okay, arms okay, fingers and toes in place. There was a bruise on his forehead and a crick in his neck but accident would not kill him, he would live to be murdered.

A bicycle light came round the corner and Romeo, armed with his gun and flashlight, arrived to check out the situation. "Anybody dead?"

Big Man swore.

And again. "You need help?"

"Pick up de fucking truck and put it back on de fucking road, you bumbo rass!"

Romeo walked round to the rear of the vehicle, shone his torch on the licence number, made a note of it, got back on his bicycle and rode away. Working for the public was a thankless task, he thought. The truck would still be there in the morning and the men would have calmed down.

At first light, Alonso knocked on the door. Romeo's wife was boiling tea.

"Mistress Foster? You know me?"

"Alonso? From long time."

"Romeo is here?"

"Asleep. He was up all night about some crash on the road."

"I know. I was in it."

145

Mrs Foster laughed.

Her children, stick-legged, crept out of the back door one by one and surrounded Alonso, staring at him.

"Tell you daddy Alonso come to see him."

Romeo appeared, zipping up his flies and buttoning his coastguard shirt with the insignia on it.

It was impossible to have a man-to-man with all those pop-eyed children and Sunny Foster's belly threatening another, so after bread and tea Romeo and Alonso repaired to the rum shop for a quarter quart. They settled on a verandah at the back of the shop which held a table and a couple of benches, fenced in by a wooden rail, giving on a view of two guinea fowl, a cactus hedge and a latrine.

"I just come from town," Alonso said airily.

"I deducted that. That's the direction the truck was pointing. I made a note to ask why, because as far as I know you are in Negril."

"I had important business in Kingston. In the course of which I made acquaintance with your auntie, Miss Mary Lou. She says to say howdy."

Romeo sighed. "Alonso, you better tell me de story properly, what you doing here, what you doing in Kingston, and what you doing with my auntie because all I know is you suspect of murder in Negril."

"You know that?"

"I know that."

"That's why I went to town, to see the Minister, Magnus Bonanza, and to ask for 'elp in my fight for innocence."

"That's how you meet up with Mary Lou?"

"Correct."

"And you think Bonanza going to help you?"

"Yes. The government firmly oppose to drugs, which was the cause and purpose of the murder."

146

Romeo decided to have his first cigarette of the day. He couldn't afford it and it was too early, but the conversation had taken a serious turn. To know something and not to say it is hard for an honest man. "True, true," he lied, "I can vouch for that. So what happen when you went to the Minister?"

"He gave me some money and he said he would work under cover and do something for me."

Romeo stayed silent. The taste of his notebook was in his mouth, but he wasn't going to spit. Not yet. "Then what happen?"

"They try to kill me."

"Who?"

"The same one kill the Chinyman."

"Alonso," Romeo sighed, indulging his pity, "who can tell you the Minister is against drugs?"

The image of Precious rose before Alonso's eyes, and with it doubt. He accused himself of idiocy, and forgave himself immediately. To be deceived by love is dangerous but no disgrace.

"Never mind," was all he said to Romeo.

"You going to lose your life if you follow that path," Romeo said. "Bonanza is in the drug business, heavily. He and an American named Leprosini, boat named *Swingtime*, are in it together. Big business. Don't ask me how I know."

"How you know?"

"I board the boat. I watch dem load at night. Between you and me, Alonso, I was going back the next morning."

"To arrest them?"

"To tell them about Lord Nelson, the famous sea dog, who clapped his telescope to his blind eye and held out his hand. But I decide to digest the information first. Luckily. There was an Indian fellow, named Maddie, witness what I witness, because he went on board next day and got a lot of money out of dem. He boast all round de village he was rich. He bathe his daughters, rub them down with oil, dress dem in silk and satin, bought them white shoes and silver bangles, proclaimed they had big dowries and took them off to town to look for husband. First day in Kingston, as he cross de street, police motorcycle knock him down and kill him. The daughters ... gone. Disappear."

"Accident? Perhaps."

"Perhaps."

"But," Alonso said, doubt hardening into certainty, "the Minister is the only man know what I know, and they fired gun at me."

"Buy me a rum," Romeo said, feeling that to save a friend's life deserved a drink. Alonso went into the shop and procured a quarter quart on the promise that the coastguard officer would pay, and they settled down for a morning of reflection. The more they drank the less they said, for the bigger the corruption the smaller the response.

"If I liberate a chicken," Alonso said at last, "is only because I hungry."

"But the chicken farmer has the right to vex."

Alonso nodded. "If I borrow a man's wife, is just for fun."

"But the man can rightfully complain," said Romeo.

"But when the man who makes the law does wrong, when the governor robs the people, that is grievous."

"Grievous," Romeo agreed. "That is when all righteous men must stay in bed."

"Easy for you, Romeo, easy to say, because you are not the murder suspeck. Powerful persons take interest in my death, an' in my silence."

"Run, boy, run."

"This is an island. Where can I run? Truth must be told so all can understand except my executioner."

12

When Precious heard about the new madman on the beach she paid it no particular mind. Madmen are common at Negril, as common as tourists. Some of them *are* tourists, like the New Yorker whose apartment door was so festooned with locks that suddenly, when he was smitten by an immense desert of water and an enclosing emptiness of air, he couldn't take it and started babbling tales of private terror to strangers on plastic cushions – endless sagas of persecution and histories of self-justification. Some of the madmen are natives, like the mountain man, bearded, dread-locked, his red mouth open in desire for the wealth of motor cruisers, pink frothy drink and naked white people. He called on God to witness Sodom and scuttled sideways across the beach to hide his head in a hole.

There was a Kingstonian in top hat and tails, umbrella in one hand and cow-cod in the other, who said his name was Joseph, and enquired politely of all and sundry if they had seen his son Jesus, who needed whipping; while an emaciated South American woman patrolled the sand in a white bathrobe showing to all who would look electric burns, abscesses, slashes and scars – the marks, she said, of torture.

Alonso, of course, was a sensible madman. He took great pains with his appearance. First he shaved his head, for baldness is the best of all disguises, changing the shape of the face, the location of the features, and the age of the hairless one, reducing him to childhood or rocketing him forward into comic strip. He was judicious in the use of paint. He imitated birds and fish and butterflies who have false features in odd places – an eye in the tail, a tail in the face – and animals who use colour to disguise their shape – a lop-sided mask or a false eyebrow well below the eye. He walked strangely. As Precious had so often compared him to a spider, he decided he would have eight legs: four of his own and four so powerfully imagined he could feel them take their turn as he crawled, backside in the sky, across the sand.

Alonso was sufficiently horrific to deter children from throwing stones at him, sufficiently pacific to keep the police from arresting him, and so bloody strange that no psychiatrist would question him. He was not conspicuous, spending long hours in the mottled shade, making his plans.

Mad and safely hidden, he still had to eat, surviving mainly on coconuts. He had rescued his machete from the pool shed at the Casuarina, and in the dead of night performed a public service all along the golden coast. The palms were not a crop, but all for show, the nuts potential menace, and Alonso climbed them monkey-like at night, carried the trophies to his lair, and feasted on their water and their meat. For variety, picnic tables yielded half-eaten hot dogs, jerk chicken bones, half-drunk beer and sour-sops only tasted.

Hunger satisfied, a spider has a certain responsibility to his genes, and the idea of Precious figured largely in Alonso's speckled hours of reflection: her perfect body, her petal skin, her two mere legs, her two mere arms, her two mere breasts, her lips, her single tongue. The shadows of his hiding place moved as the spider's body sighed for her, but he did not dare approach Precious or the Casuarina kitchen. The thought of a white Toyota van and a hail of bullets kept him secret still.

He would not go to Precious so Precious came to him, sailing down the beach in her blue uniform and white pinafore. As she was always on duty, she must have sneaked away to meet a man, the spider thought. She was carrying her shoes in her hand, keeping to the soft dry sand by the sea grapes which emphasised every step she took, like a dancer in slow motion. She passed quite close to Alonso, her uniform crisp and starched, her lips parted, breathing the sea air.

Alonso scurried through a maze of bushes, tracking her. She went only as far as the canoe, the rotting canoe with the hole in it, their private place, their bedchamber. There was no man there, she was meeting breeze. He watched in hiding as Precious sat on the canoe, looking out to sea. She sang a little song but he could not catch the words. They sounded like 'Moon over Miami' … and then she squeezed a little salt water from her eyes, which she dashed away with the back of her hand.

This was too much for Alonso. "Precious," he whispered, "it's me."

"Well, I don't know why I'm bawlin' for you," she said, as if the voice had been inside her head. "You only gone to Kingston, you not dead."

"As good as dead," came the mutter from the sea grapes, and she turned to see a shaven-headed meagre man, crouched, looking at her with alligator eyes.

Precious jumped. "You frighten me! You are the new madman! You! What kind of damn foolishness you up to now, Alonso? You mad, you know, you mad, mad, mad, stark staring mad! What you think you look like, you strikin' hignorant brute!"

This was the same woman who had just been squirting salt water for the love of him, Alonso thought. Which one of them was mad?

"Precious," he said soberly, getting out of his spider crouch and sitting cross-legged on the sand, "this is a disguise. I has to live incognito as I am a murder suspeck wanted by the law and, worse than that, hunted by the criminal element."

"What happen with Bonanza?"

"That's him. The criminal element. The Minister arrange for me to die."

151

"You mad?"

"I look mad?"

"Yes."

"Well, is true."

"True dat you mad?"

"True dat de Minister order it."

"No."

Precious thought about it, wiggling her toes in the sand, while he watched the emotions chasing each other across her face, love routed by doubt, fear replaced by anger and, finally, by determination. "The Minister comin' here again."

"When?"

"Day after."

"How you know?"

"Is written down. Booked. I going to ask him. Straight. Mr Bonanza, what is your word on the drug business? You lie to me? You tell me propaganda? What you going to do about my man, Alonso?"

"Precious," said the madman with the white paint across his nose, "I beg you. I beg you don't do it! Don't mention me unless you mourn, unless you want to mourn for true. Trus' me, Precious. If you ask for mercy from a man, he will be merciless. I goin' find a way to pop him, to tangle him in his net. Precious, I beg you, shut your mout'!"

"Well, is your life an' I not interes' in it," she said, straightened her knees, brushed the sand off her skirt and swayed lazily up the beach as if nothing in the world mattered but how she looked as she walked away.

"Magnus Bonanza coming," thought the spider in the sea-grapes. "Him smart, me smarter. Him smart, me smarter." He thought and thought, and thought of nothing.

But next morning, when he opened his eye and pointed it toward the sea, he saw *Swingtime's* white hull beyond the reef, seeking an opening, finding it, moving slowly without movement, drifting abreast the Casuarina, splashing an anchor in, and swinging on the chain to rest, head to the northeast breeze.

Selwyn and Stephen, separate and inseparable, stayed on board. Carlotta came ashore. *Swingtime's* room at the Casuarina, number 97, was permanently reserved. Throwing her sailing bag on one of the twin beds, Carlotta was reminded again that she'd been fired. Leprosini, flying off, had told her to do the same: to disappear into the English mist, go back to a sense of failure, to cold sheets and unemployment. She went on the balcony to contemplate the sea through a fan of palm leaves. They shivered in the light wind, giving glimpses of the yacht, property of the accursed tycoon. She wanted this place – the warmth, the blue, the green, life in a bathing suit, meals for a signature, drinks for a smile, plumbing that sometimes worked, electric light, black people treating her like royalty; she wanted all of it without Leprosini. She wanted God's creation without God. Blasphemy!

Maybe he wouldn't come; some convulsion of the Han Sen, an Irish bomb, a car crash or a sick sudden passion for a teenage boy would change his mind, delay him, bury him under tons of rock or water. Wishful thinking!

She had to decide whether, when Leprosini came, she would ask his forgiveness, slip her knickers off and lie down resigned, or rescue her dog-eared return from the bottom of her purse, repack her sailing bag and ask Mass George for a lift to the airport. She'd think about it tomorrow.

A beach towel round her shoulders, barefoot, she went down the stairs, along the covered walk and through the patio, passing the recovered zinnias on which Chin Lee had expired, through the hotel in view of the diners, heading toward the beach. A gentleman from St Louis who fancied himself a connoisseur of knees, choked on his ice water. Oblivious, Carlotta found her favourite lounger, stretched out and closed her eyes.

She was not sure how long she'd been there when a deep whisper in her ear said, "When de boss man comin'?"

Carlotta was not the screaming type and she'd been to Negril before, so she was not surprised, opening her eyes, to see Alonso, shaved, painted, on all fours, his torso bare, his loins just covered in a pair of guest-left jeans.

"Why do you want to know?"

"Answer me first."

"I don't know."

"Me nor. But he comin'?"

"That's the idea."

"You waitin' for him?"

"Tell me something," Carlotta said, rising on one elbow. "Why do you want to know? What is your interest in Leprosini? Are you selling something?"

"Suppose I ask you the same question, Miss Carlotta. What you selling?" the madman replied.

That was a slap in the face from an unexpected hand.

"I'd rather not discuss it with you," Carlotta said, taking refuge in her English accent.

"No shame," Alonso said, magnanimous. "Money want a pretty woman."

"Yes," she said bitterly.

"Pretty woman want money. Fair swap."

Carlotta did not comment. Alonso, with the licence of insanity, pressed on. "You can't complain, you can buy everything! Drive car! Fly plane! Read magazine! Wear diamonds and ruby jewels! Drink wine, smoke cigarette an' watch Sky television!"

"All that is true," Carlotta said, "but I hate him. He makes me actually, physically, sick."

Alonso scratched a place behind his ear where the dry paint itched, and Carlotta noticed that the raised arm rippled his shoulder muscles, each one outlined clear as an anatomy lesson. "You must never talk to people," Alonso said philosophically. "You think people happy and they tell you sadness; you think they good, they tell you badness; and those that you consider wise just tell you foolishness. Miss Carlotta, you has beauty, you deserve a rich man."

"Haven't I seen you before?" Carlotta interrupted.

"I jus' drop down from Mars," he said, remembering he was supposed to be mad.

"Did you ever have anything to do with stainless steel tubes?"

"No, not me."

"Yes, you."

"Okay, you tell me what was inside de parrots."

Carlotta was caught and Alonso took his life in his hands. "De fact is, dey arrest me fo' de murder of Chin Lee an' I has no one to help me, save you. What was in de parrots?"

"Your guess is as good as mine."

"I guess cocaine."

She said nothing, her attention distracted by a pelican diving.

Alonso tried again. "When de big boss comin'?"

"I don't know."

"But him comin'?"

"Yes."

"Why?"

"For the same reason he goes anywhere: to do deals."

"In *you-ess*?"

"What?"

"In *you-ess* dollars?"

"Inevitably."

Alonso made himself comfortable, lying back and scratching his stomach where the jeans were tight. The muscles of his stomach wall were ridged like a Roman breastplate. Lying on the sand beside her, he reminded her of her favourite man, the dying Gaul in the Capitoline Museum in Rome.

"So ... if you don't like the man," Alonso said, "all you has to do is get a richer one."

Carlotta hugged her knees, pulling them up against her breasts. "What about a poor one?" she asked, innocent.

"No good," Alonso said, "no good. That's a bad swap. You must swap beauty fo' wealth. A woman is God's greatest beauty an' mus' not go cheap." He looked up at her, the beach towel draped around her shoulders, falling in love with her, confusing, as men do, beauty for wisdom, fear for compassion.

"Like a waterfall," he said.

She smiled.

"I know a waterfall," Alonso went on, "over the hill yonder, where I used to go ... where de river tumble down into a pool an' de water is all white an' full of noise; but if you dive down into de pool an' swim against the current, and dive again, you go underneat' de fall of water an' come up in a secret cave, an' you stay dere, hiding behind the curtain of the waterfall, peaceful ... sweet."

Carlotta was moved, wondering what it would be like with a man who thought so highly, so tenderly of woman, and was, in his own way, so strong. She was not wanton, only idly curious and, in the hot sunshine, bold. She touched his shoulder, a patch of skin where the paint had flaked. It was very soft, and hard, like steel cables wrapped in thin silk. "You've almost no subcutaneous fat," she sighed.

156

Precious, who had come behind them, with order pad and tray, felt this had gone far enough. "Go 'way," she cried. "Go 'way, boy. You t'ink you can jus' come on de hotel beach and moles' de touris' like dat? Get your backside off de beach! I call Madame Juliette, Mass George an' all police on you! Go 'way!" she shouted.

"It's all right, Precious," Carlotta cooed. "We were having an interesting conversation. He wasn't bothering me. Whoever he is, he's not as mad as he looks."

Precious was not mollified. "He's much more mad, ma'am! Go 'way!" And she kicked sand in Alonso's face. "I'll give you waterfall! Get!"

Alonso fled, forgetting his eight legs, remembering at least to howl and flap.

***

That night the spider borrowed a bar of soap from the hotel laundry and set about removing the paint, scrubbing himself with sand, washing in the sea and, as there was no watchman to prevent it, rinsing under the freshwater shower on the beach. Dressed in his old T-shirt and khaki trousers, recognisable once more as Alonso, even to the whistle on a cord around his neck, he set off at dawn to return to Mountain Valley.

Security was tighter now and the birdcalls started when he was three miles away. Cheekily, he answered them, giving his famous imitation of a solitaire, and the birds led him through the village, past Miss Kelly's grocery store and the Baptist Church, and half a mile further on to a new compound in a grove of sweetwood trees, their stems covered in great creepers forming a rampart like a castle wall. On a platform perched in one of them, a machine gun pointed at him. Ras had either become more efficient or more ingenious in finding uses for the weapons he was accumulating.

Alonso, whistling, followed a worn pathway through the trees, past abandoned tins, broken bottles, bits of twine and rain-soaked plastic packaging. Eventually, he came upon Ras, swinging in a hammock, his pipe full of sacred weed. Sundry of his men, the Army of Jah, were busy resting in the neighbourhood.

Ras took a while to recognise him. The eagle eyes blinked slow and then he screeched. "Alonso! You de murderer dat ran away! You look dead?"

The sound alerted the freedom fighters who were on duty, that is to say awake, and in due time, gathered. Alonso, surrounded, kept his silence.

"What you come for?" Ras demanded, sitting up in his hammock.

"Hungry. I hungry."

Ras chuckled, shaking all over with delight. "Hungry, him say, de man him come because him hungry! Meagre man, if I cut you throat, you belly don't talk again."

"Yes, sir, hungry," repeated Alonso, piteously.

"We better feed him first and kill him after. Gi' 'im something to eat!"

A future national hero, evidently in charge of grub, disappeared into a bamboo shed built to keep the rain off the cooking pots, and returned with an enamel soup plate in which a piece of breadfruit and a boiled green banana swam in a purple soup with the black remnants of a fish's fin. Alonso gobbled it all down, pausing to smile his gratitude at the ring of surly faces watching him. When the plate was shining clean, he returned it to his benefactor, licked his fingers, and addressed himself once more to Ras. "One good turn deserves another."

Ras was not impressed. He merely stared, watching Alonso shift from foot to foot and then continue.

"You tell me some time ago, you goin' to do something big, something famous beyond Jamaica, makin' de name of Ras Clawt known around de world."

"Is known."

"For selling ganja, robbin' touris' and cutting phone line."

"Is known."

"Not much. You never lead the army out on a big battle plan."

"In time," Ras said, "when de time is ripe."

"I come to tell you de time ripe now because you are in danger. People plotting to bring you down. Jamaica minister and CIA meeting to plot combine exercise against you, while you sleeping in the bush."

Ras Clawt got out of the hammock. "A'right ... slow ... slow ..." He walked around Alonso as if by looking at the back of the watchman's head he might read what was inside. "Who plottin'? What?"

The bait was taken and Alonso paid out the line. "Magnus Bonanza, Minister of Trade ..."

"Crook."

"Marco Leprosim."

"Crook."

"The CIA."

Ras put his face as close to Alonso's as the difference in height would allow and grinned mirthlessly, showing his gums. "I do business with the CIA all de time. They are not agains' me. I sell dem stuff, dey give me guns. I am anti-communis'. I believe in market forces. Is well known."

"This is different CIA," Alonso whispered, giving away a secret.

"This CIA mean 'Christ is American'. This is a serious gang of people, man. They rule America an' dey mean to rule de world. This man is one of dem, an' he comin' to overtake

Jamaica. You are de stumbling block, an' dey mus' destroy you. You want to know de plot?"

"No."

"Okay. I won't tell you. Let me go."

"Since you walk so far, you might as well. What is de plot?"

"To starve you out! No more breadfruit and boil' banana, no jerk pig, no stamp an' go nor dip an' fall back, no ackee, sal' fish, shad, no curry goat, no rice an' peas, no coconut oil, no janga in de river, no patty. CIA say you mus' eat slice' bread and Macdonald burgers an' you mus' tek you money and go an buy Kentucky Fry. Firs' starve and den defoliate. CIA will spray all ganja fields wid poison and kill de sacred weed. They will ex'ume Bob Marley an' scatter him to de wind."

Ras spat.

"Birt' control," Alonso said, portentously, and all the freedom fighters twitched.

"They putting substance in de water, an' de air, and spreading substance on de food to weaken black man sperm. They goin' tie rubber bag upon your prick an' interfere wid women. Birt' control is de plan to kill nayga man so only white will live, worldwide."

Ras was beginning to look worried. It sounded plausible.

"And Aids," Alonso said. "They take our 'ealthy mothers' boys as migrant workers, hide dem from women, ship dem to Florida, Louisiana, infeck dem an' fly dem backwards to Jamaica as Aids-carrying batty men. Soon all black will meagre, rot and die across de lengt' and breadt'!"

It was a terrifying prophecy and Ras reacted violently. "Alonso, you are a lying bumbo-rass!" he squeaked and squealed. "How do you know? Tell me how you know or I will kill you dead!" and he approached Alonso, towering over him, holding a machete above his head.

"'Oman tell me. English 'oman tell me."

"Why?"

Alonso smiled a modest smile and the machete was lowered.

"You, meagre man?"

Alonso nodded.

"She mus' be ol' an fat."

"No. She young and sweet. An' she looking to see you."

"The whore of Babylon! The scarlet 'oman!"

"No, boss, is only friendly she friendly. Dat's why she tell me de plot."

"Plot?" Quick thinking does not mix with cannabis and Ras was beginning to lag behind.

"The plot to kill nayga!"

"Sweet an' friendly. Respectable!"

"Don't think about de 'oman. Consider your glory."

"What is glory?"

"You will defeat the CIA."

"Uh-huh."

"You must strike first."

"Yeah, man."

"If you strike first, you got him."

"Yeah, man."

"I, Alonso, has a plan."

13

It was late at night, and there was no malice in Madame Juliette's choice of room for Fonseca. She checked the plan, saw 111 was empty, asked Precious if the sheets were clean and handed her the key. Fonseca, carrying his own bag, followed the girl across the patio, burglar-lit. As she mounted the stairs in front of him, Fonseca reminded himself of the dangers of propositioning staff, and so did not notice until the door closed behind him that he was in Chin Lee's room. His bag did not touch the floor. He hurried back across the patio and confronted the *patronne* as she pulled down the shutters on the bar. "I can't stay in that room."

"What's wrong, Mr Fonseca?"

"I can smell the cesspit."

"You can smell the end of your nose, I think," Madame Juliette said scornfully. She wasn't going to stand for any of that.

"Tell me the truth, sir. What's the matter?"

"I said it's dirty. It smells. Something wrong with the lav."

She was about to wake Mass George, who had gone to bed after a hard day. His sciatica was bothering him and, being Jamaican, he always found tripe *à la mode de Caen* slow to digest and needed to lie down. George would sort out this croaking lizard. Then she remembered. "You came here some time back, Mr Fonseca?"

"Yes, I've been here before."

"About the time we had an accident in that room?"

"Oh, was it? Yes."

"Why didn't you say so? You're superstitious. Don't worry. I promise you, Chinese do not have ghosts. If they did, the

162

world would be overpopulated with ectoplasm. The room is clean and safe, and the hotel is full. But if you prefer, you can go down to the Green Flash. Aids put them out of business and they are always empty."

Fonseca grasped the nettle, took the key and headed for the car park where Bullfrog sat asleep at the wheel of the Toyota. He shook the squashed man awake. "Come, you sleeping inside."

"Is okay, man. I 'custom to sleep here."

"Do what I tell you, c'mon."

Grumbling and cursing, Bullfrog followed.

The two villains were installed in the twin beds of 111, stretched on their racks, waiting for torture. Bullfrog, who had no nerves, slept comfortably, but Fonseca lay awake, listening to the sound of Chin Lee's skull cracking like a peanut shell.

***

Up in the mountains Ras stood under a waterfall, clearing his head, preparing for battle. Alonso, deputised to whip him, flogged him with a guava switch until he grunted, to wake his sleeping senses and to rouse his anger. Then, in the night, Ras moved among his men from hammock to hammock, confiscating ganja. Alonso followed him, meekly, carrying a krukus bag for the weed. "You name on it," he said to each and all. "I keep it safe."

"They mus' taste no joy tonight," Ras explained, "for tomorrow I want lions. You know your Bible, Alonso?"

"Somewhat," Alonso replied cautiously.

"Then you know how Gideon does select his soldier for battle. He sen' back all de weak-back, all de coward, all de greedy man, an' he keep only de man who can lap water out of his hand an' look over him shoulder at de same time. Remember dat one?"

"If you test dem like dat, it might be only you an' me dat go to war," Alonso said.

"Leastways we are not stoned. We will fight bloodily until deat'."

"Right, right," Alonso said.

"Put de krukus bag under your head and keep it there."

So saying Ras stretched out to sleep, choosing a stony place in the open air. Above him the moon played hide and seek among the black clouds, flashing like a celestial lighthouse guiding him to glory. Alonso kept under cover, his head on the krukus bag as ordered, its soft aroma giving him sweet dreams of precious things.

***

Magnus Bonanza arrived in the late morning, accompanied by Miss Pearl, a detective and a chauffeur. He had decided to come by limousine, stopping overnight in Montego Bay to be entertained by businessmen, rather than fly direct by Island Hopper. The Hopper had no first class accommodation, not even a nylon curtain like those carried by Air Jamaica to conceal politicians. Magnus had made a point of it to Island Hopper, who, knowing that Magnus never paid his fare, refused to install a partition of any sort.

But he arrived, the purpose of his visit undeclàred, his entourage discreet. The detective set about his duties, reading the register, clocking the shrubbery in the patio and the girls on the beach. The chauffeur handed over the luggage and took the limousine into Negril to impress a woman he hoped was still there, while Bonanza and Miss Pearl made for the watering place.

"Pearl, if the ministry could manage a bar in the back of the car it would make long journeys like this more palatable."

"Bad propaganda," Pearl said disapprovingly and asked Precious for lemonade. "Fresh lime, do you hear? I don't want any gas."

"Appleton Gold ... and ginger," Bonanza said, smiling at her. "Don't I remember you?"

"I hope so, Minister," Precious replied darkly.

"What do you mean?" Bonanza said hastily, fearing a sexual involvement he had forgotten. Miss Pearl gave Precious a searching look, classifying and cataloguing her.

Precious was about to reply when she noticed Madame Juliette in frog position behind the cash register, watching her, so she merely smiled and went off to get the drinks.

Bonanza was aware of unfinished business and, conspiratorial by nature, he knew that it was secret. He waited for Miss Pearl's bladder to fill or Madame Juliette to smell something burning in the kitchen, but neither happened. All the long pre-lunch drinking session he was aware of Precious, and not because of her rounded shape and general attraction but because of the undisguised menace in her eye.

At the fourth drink order, he threw caution to the winds. "Why you remember me, darling?"

"Dis is not de firs' time you come, Minister."

"Yes, yes," impatiently.

"So what happen," she asked, "to de big development? We did expeck bulldozer tearing up de place by now."

"Oh, that," Bonanza laughed. "Yes, it's coming. Rome was not built in a day. First, you must have plans, contracts and licences."

"Licence for what, sir?"

There was something about her tone Bonanza didn't like. It was aggressive, almost disrespectful.

"You wouldn't understand, darling. Just get me a drink."

"I understand when people dead and when people gone to jail!"

"People?"

165

"My friend."

"Your friend?"

"The watchman."

"Ah … there is no connection," Bonanza assured her, and added, with maximum sincerity, "I can promise you that."

Miss Pearl shifted uneasily. "I'm going to wash my hands for lunch. Don't bother with the lemonade." She waddled away, a duck in a cream two-piece suit.

"Get the rum," Bonanza said, losing patience, but Precious stood her ground.

"I heard you in this very bar, sitting over there, I heard you declaring policy against drug smugglin' and how you would hang all o' dem."

"True, true … just get the rum." Bonanza had come to the end of his tether. It was just too much to have to defend his record to a member of the public, a person with no money. He looked over towards Madame Juliette, smiled and shrugged, a semaphore that read, "Call off your staff, I'm only here for a drink."

Precious saw the signal and decided on an adjournment. "We'll talk again, sir. I don't satisfy," she said, and left.

Bonanza's eyes followed her and he wondered how so much controlled venom could lurk in such a body, and he regretted the lies a man was forced to tell to maintain some semblance of democracy.

***

The Army of Jah was on the move: twenty-five foot soldiers, Ras, the general, and Alonso, political adviser. They looked like mountain men going to market or coming to watch a cricket match or aiming to join a jump-up. Six donkeys teetered in the midst of them, their tiny hooves negotiating the rain-scoured, rutted road. On their flanks, large hampers, flapping like their ears, were crammed with palm thatch –

166

mere camouflage concealing guns and ammunition supplied by the Peace Corps.

At the main road Ras ordered a halt and deployed them skilfully about the bush.

***

Carlotta, alone at a table for two, was thinking about Alonso. She had a soft spot for the watchman, tube manufacturer or painted spider. In the conversation about the waterfall and in his outright disapproval of her behaviour she recognised a part of herself that was dying, the urge to rebel for nameless principle, the wish to survive on her own terms, to enjoy life without compromise or self-hatred. But Alonso had the advantage of her, she thought; he had nothing, nothing to lose, and so could live according to his lights. She envied him and wanted him to comfort her, to approve of her so she might approve of herself.

Across the terrace, crowded with bright beach shirts, red and white bodies, hibiscus blossoms in little vases, half-eaten lunches, lurid drinks and her friends the cling-clings foraging for crumbs, Carlotta could see the Minister and Miss Pearl lunching in the dark interior, not seeking the sun or publicity. The sight of them rang a tiny warning bell in her brain and gave her a little shot of adrenalin to counter her habitual gloom. "Something's up," she said to herself.

"You want lunch?" Precious said, putting down the iced water.

"I wish you could lunch with me, Precious. I'm lonely."

"Thank you," smiled Precious. "Next time. So what you want, the usual grated carrot and diet mayonnaise?"

"What else is there?"

"Lobster. Out of the sea this mawnin'. Grilled lobster tail in melted butter. Very nice."

"Lobster is an endangered species."

"Sorry?"

"In danger of becoming extinct."

"Getting very scarce," Precious agreed.

"Then maybe I shouldn't."

"Not to worry; this one dead a'ready."

"Where's the madman?"

"Gone."

"Do you know where he went?"

"No."

"And if you knew, you wouldn't tell me."

"I wouldn't tell anybody."

"I'll have the lobster."

"Yes. Best keep body and soul together," Precious said and departed.

Her place was taken by Fonseca, the upright alligator, who had the cheek to pull up a chair and sit with her unbidden. Carlotta regarded him with a level stare. The Minister here, she thought, and now Fonseca. It was only a matter of time.

"I didn't invite you to sit there," Carlotta said, in the voice that ruled India.

"What have you got against me?"

"I want to be alone."

"Do you know what it's like, Miss Carlotta, to be hated by women? I love them, pretty ones especially," and he smiled, "but to a man, they hate me. They think I'm slimy, ugly, they say I have no manners, no sex appeal, that I'm creepy and sadistic ..."

"Do you have a wife, Mr Fonseca?"

"Yes. She doesn't like me either."

"Never?"

"Oh, for a spell, years ago, you know. I suppose the breeding instinct had hold of her. Anybody can look good under the influence of that."

"I'd prefer to eat alone."

"Okay," Fonseca said, getting to his feet. "When's Marco coming? He told me to be here."

"I don't know," Carlotta said, looking out to sea. Fonseca followed her look. The red rubber dinghy was casting off from *Swingtime*, and with a spurt of the engine they could hear from shore and a quarter circle of white wake, it was coming to the beach, avoiding the black heads of the swimmers and the large bodies of the waders to slide up the sand toward the topless persons. Selwyn, the hairy one, and Stephen, the ginger man, jumped out, secured the outboard and pulled the red doughnut clear of the water.

They spotted Carlotta under the coconut tree, waved to her and came towards her. Stephen, bare-chested, his floppy hat shading his face, saluted Fonseca, and Selwyn, knife at his belt, sat down beside him. "Three o'clock, Fonseca. Have the Toyota waiting."

"That's the answer to your question, Fonseca. You can go now," Carlotta said.

Fonseca did.

Just then Precious appeared with the lobster.

"The condemned man ate a hearty breakfast," Selwyn said, admiring it.

"What are you two doing on shore?"

"He said he wanted witnesses."

"Who said?"

"Leprosini, on the radio."

"Witnesses!"

"He said, 'Is that limey bitch still there?'"

"We said, 'Carlotta, of whom we are very fond, is still a member of the crew, yes.' He said he wanted witnesses, he wanted us in the next room."

"Why don't you boys share the lobster?" Carlotta said, trembling. "I think I'm the endangered species."

***

A man named Zekiel driving an open truck loaded with chickens, coming up a steep incline in low gear, was surprised to see what looked like a thatched roof sheltering donkeys right in the middle of the road. He stood on the brake, and leaned on the horn, stuck his head out the window and shouted, "Get off de road, you stupid nayga!"

Little did he know what he had said and, in fact, he never knew because a freedom fighter jumped off the bank and took his head off with a machete.

The chickens, the decapitated driver and the donkeys were all hidden in the bush and the army, now equipped with modern transport, resumed its march.

Approaching Negril, two supermarkets, a bar and a round-about signal civilisation. The truck turned right, scorning the town, and crossed the bridge over the river. This so-called river, mostly dry, was only the overflow of the swamp in heavy rain but it was Alonso's Rubicon, for the police station and Detective Inspector Swaby were now behind him, between the Army and a retreat to Mountain Valley. The Casuarina Hotel lay ahead and there was no turning back.

Bouncing in the body of the truck, looking over the rust-flecked cab, he saw the silver bullet of Leprosini's plane settling into Sunset Strip. "Das him," he said to Ras, pointing. "Dat is de Yankee-Christ!"

14

A man in a blue suit sat in the corner and said nothing. He had a hand-painted tie, shiny black shoes and soft hands. His barber was a little old-fashioned but he was clean-shaven and exuded French scent. Carlotta, white trousers and a flowered shirt hiding her charms, was delegated to pour champagne. Marco Leprosini, affability itself, a stallion rampant on his sweat-shirted chest, was so glad to see his friends, to get together with guys he loved, people on whom his operation depended, employees he cared about, and who made him feel real good.

Nobody except Carlotta actually liked champagne, and Leprosini stuck to mineral water, but everybody else was drinking it, even Mass George and Madame Juliette, who had been summoned to room 97 to celebrate the millionaire's arrival. Selwyn and Stephen sipped theirs on the balcony, keeping the boat in view and avoiding conversation.

Carlotta had unpacked the bags, all but one, which was too large for a briefcase, too small for clothing, with combination locks and corners reinforced. This bag lay on Leprosini's bed, and the man in the blue suit never took his eyes off it.

Bonanza arrived without Miss Pearl, beaming and back-slapping, and asking Leprosini about his trip. Under cover of this, the proprietors made their excuses and departed. Carlotta gave Bonanza a glass of bubbly and, forcing it down, he went on questioning his friend Marco about such things as the Euro, the price of oil and the exchange rate on the US dollar. Leprosini said they were all terrific and moved to the black bag. Conversation paused.

"Shit," said Leprosini, "I forgot. I left that thing in Miami," and he laughed.

Bonanza was not laughing. "I don't think so," he said. "If you did, you might not leave Jamaica alive."

"I'm kidding," said Leprosini. "You know I'm a man of my word. Nobody makes it in business without trust."

The man in the blue suit put his hand in his pocket and took out an envelope which he handed to Leprosini, who handed it in turn to Bonanza. "Deposit slip, National Savings, Grand Cayman. Okay?"

Stephen and Selwyn on the balcony were absorbed in the setting of the sun, seeing no evil, hearing no evil, but Carlotta watched Bonanza open the envelope, and waited while Bonanza fought to control his anger, breathing heavily and biting his lip. Leprosini had turned his back on the Minister, refreshing his Perrier, indicating the business was over.

"This is not what we agreed," Bonanza said huskily.

"Don't I know it! That's something to be taken care of, real quick. Coupl'a weeks! There's a little problem with the cash flow, you know. Some of my people in New York are paying late. You've never heard so many excuses. It's incredible! I said to them, 'What are you guys doing? Supplying shit on credit?' But Magnus, what I've given you there is not bad, not bad at all. I mean, I wish I was as rich as you are. You've got it made!"

"This is not what we agreed."

"Are you going to do something about it?" said Leprosini, and the man in the blue suit shuffled his feet.

Magnus Bonanza placed his champagne glass carefully down on the coffee table. "I don't drink piss, not with a shit," he said.

"Hey, hey, hey!" Leprosini protested. "C'mon, you'll get the rest. We'll talk about it after dinner. I'm buying dinner. Look, Magnus, friendship is important to me, more important than money. Come on. That's the best I could do at this moment in time. You'll get the rest. I'm an honest man."

"Okay," Bonanza said. "We'll talk later."

Leprosini waited until he was down the staircase and out of earshot, and then he grinned at Carlotta. "That's all he's ever going to get, the black son-of-a-bitch. That's all he's worth. Politicians come cheaper and cheaper, you know that." Leprosini turned to the next item on the agenda.

"Stephen."

"Sir."

"Selwyn."

"Sir."

The crew came in from the balcony. Leprosini was fiddling with the combination on the bag until the locks sprang open, and he lifted the lid to reveal stacks and stacks of used banknotes – American dollars in small denominations. "Kids' lunch money," he said with a winning smile. "From the streets of New York. What do I owe you?"

"Six months," Stephen said.

"Here, count it yourself." Leprosini threw money at him, and Stephen, the man who wanted to run a green home for deprived children, carefully counted out the soiled and crumpled bills, sorting the tens from the fives and the ones from the twenties until he had achieved his wages. He handed the rest back to Leprosini.

"You can keep the change," the drug baron said.

"I'd rather not," Stephen replied with dignity, hoping for a small victory in defeat.

Selwyn, in training for corporate fraud, had no such compunction. His counting was quick, inaccurate and erred in his favour.

"That leaves the two creeps."

"And Carlotta."

"She gets hers later." Leprosini took two sealed envelopes from the case. "They're in room 111. Take these over there Stephen."

"No, thanks."

"What do you mean?"

"If you're pulling something on them, I'd rather not be the messenger."

"What's going on around here? Nobody trusts me." Leprosini was enjoying himself. "Look, nobody cheats a hit man. You pay in full. Or you cancel him altogether."

The man in the blue suit tried to smile, and failed.

"Why don't we sleep on it," Leprosini said after a pause, "and pay them tomorrow."

***

The stolen truck had been cached in an empty lot, obscured by a billboard that said 'Crescent Cottages Coming Soon', and the Army of Jah had melted into the sea-grapes. Ras and Alonso held a whispered council of war. Ras thought delay was dangerous; he thought they should storm the place in a hail of bullets, shoot everybody in sight and set the hotel on fire. Alonso thought this was a brilliant plan, but it lacked subtlety and had a disadvantage. Such an attack could not be kept secret for long, and would invite counter-attack. If it were possible, he suggested, to achieve the objective and get back to Mountain Valley before anybody knew what had happened ...

"You mean kill nobody at all!"

"The odd one or two."

Ras was silent, thinking.

Alonso pursued his drift. He knew the habits of the hotel. At ten, the dining room closed; at midnight, the bar. Children were asleep by nine, Mass George by ten, bridge players by eleven, drunks by half past twelve, Madame Juliette by one o'clock, and Precious ...

"You want to attack like a t'ief, not a soldier."

"T'ief live longer," Alonso said. He volunteered to go in at half past ten to immobilise Mass George's fog horn. At eleven Ras could do what he knew how to do, and at half past Alonso would raid the store room for kerosene and empty Coca-Cola bottles, and on leaving, pull out all the fuses in the electricity supply.

"Then what?" said Ras.

***

Leprosini pulled off the sweatshirt with the rampant stallion to reveal his handsome torso. His shoulders were athletically broad and well-muscled. A gold medallion dangled between his sculpted pectorals. The tan was almost Mediterranean, but being fair-skinned, he freckled. His triceps were a trifle loose, denying him perfection, and his racket forearm was larger than its twin. He had a waistline, and gold tinted hair in his cleavage and on his stomach above the navel. "Carlotta," he said.

Carlotta, on the balcony, her back to him, seemed not to have heard.

"Get in here."

Carlotta glanced at the next balcony where Stephen and Selwyn, in their pyjamas, were looking at the sea. Stephen looked back at her and gave her a thumbs-up sign, wishing her luck. She ignored him and entered the bedroom. "You've got your audience," she said.

"Got to give the little queers a thrill," he said. "Get ready."

Carlotta, still in her white trousers and flowered shirt, sat on the bed, propped a pillow behind her back and crossed one leg over the other.

"Bitch," he said, and went into the bathroom. Carlotta listened to the splashing and the patting, the gargling and the spraying, and wondered how many people were in there. She

175

looked around for something to read and found only a copy of *The Watchtower*, a publication new to her. This is fascinating stuff, she thought, clutching at straws, but after a page or two she thought maybe it would be better to give up the unequal struggle, stop trying to make sense of it all, and join the lunatics, who at least were sure. She looked up to see Leprosini standing at the foot of the bed in his cream silk pyjama trousers.

"I'm going to fuck you until you scream."

Carlotta considered this proposition calmly; her legs remained crossed and *The Watchtower* stayed in her hand. "It's so big," she said clearly. "Oh, my God, it's enormous!"

"Get your clothes off!"

"Oh yes ... yes ... yes!" she said, without moving.

Leprosini sat down on the bed and picked up the telephone. He dialled, and Carlotta, thinking this might be her salvation, made a lot of moaning noises for the benefit of Selwyn and Stephen, and beat her fists on the bed. After what seemed an age, Leprosini was connected, it seemed, to someone named Sandra.

After an introduction on the frigidity of English women, he asked Sandra what she was doing. Sandra, on cue, launched into a lurid description of something or other, which so excited Leprosini that his racquet hand strayed inside his cream silk. What Sandra was saying Carlotta couldn't quite hear, but judging by Leprosini's moans, groans and cries of encouragement, it was certainly working for him. Then Carlotta realised that Leprosini was telling Sandra what she, Carlotta, was doing to him, which she wasn't, she was reading *The Watchtower*.

Annoyed, Carlotta, taking her life in her hands, leaned over the side of the bed, and pulled the telephone cord out of the socket.

"Fuck!" said Leprosini loudly, jiggling the hook. "This fucking country!"

"Oh, has the line gone dead?" Carlotta said. "Oh, dear."

Sexually frustrated, unable to make a telephone call, Leprosini faced a terrible night. Sleep was impossible. There was no television, or radio, and he hadn't the intellectual curiosity for *The Watchtower*. Carlotta was adding insult to injury by sleeping peacefully in the nude. Leprosini did some exercises – deep-breathing, leg-lifting, press-ups – then took his vitamin pills, cleaned his teeth again and got into bed with his pocket calculator.

The bedside light went out. Shit. First he thought it was the bulb, then a fuse, then, from the blackness outside his window, the complete darkness of the tropics without even the comfort of a burglar light, he decided it must be a power cut. Fucking inefficient backward country. Too hot to sleep. Carlotta shifted in bed and made a little whimpering sound like someone having a pleasant dream. He could hear the wavelets on the goddam beach, the crickets and the cackling tree toads, and on the ceiling little phosphorescent green lights were blinking on and off. Devils' arseholes. It was hell.

Light moved on the ceiling and he heard muffled voices, threatening and quarrelling voices in a dialect he could not understand. Savages. It sounded like a gathering of gorillas. Leprosini got out of bed and looked down into the patio garden. Torches moved back and forth, and unseen men were shouting at one another. Sure as shit they weren't from the electric company. Some kind of voodoo ceremony. He heard a distinctly American voice cry, "What the fuck's going on!" then a burst of automatic fire, a woman screaming, and then silence.

Leprosini started to get dressed. Carlotta was out of bed, crawling toward the balcony. "Stephen," she said quietly.

"I'm here."

"The telephone's gone, and the lights."

"I'm going to the boat."

In the reflected light from the sea, she saw him go over the balcony rail, hang by his hands, fall into the sand and disappear.

Ten seconds later, there was a shout and a rattle of gunfire.

"Oh, my God," Carlotta whispered.

The bedroom door was kicked open, and black men with bottle torches and automatic rifles crowded into the room.

Alonso's voice said, "Dat's him, dat's Leprosini," and another voice, a strange high fluting voice, said, "Pussy!"

Carlotta, not wanting to draw attention to herself, reached for her clothing, which was lying on the bed.

The high voice said, "If you move, sweetheart, somebody goin' shoot you."

"I'm getting dressed," she said, with great authority, and the men, holding fire, watched her.

Ras laughed, "Alonso, is dis de pussy dat tell you 'bout de CIA?"

"A different one," Alonso said hastily, for he liked Carlotta. "Is a different one waiting fo' you."

"Dis one sweet."

"Respectable."

"Oh Lawd!"

"No time now, man."

"Plenty time. Bwoys, tie up Mr Leprosy and dump him."

The terrified Leprosini, who had hoped to be forgotten in the moment of fascination caused by Carlotta, felt himself seized by the men, who stank of sweat and chicken shit. His arms were pinned behind his back and a noose placed loosely around his neck, the long end of which was in the hands of an evil-looking brute, the sort who would tighten it for fun.

"Pussy!" Ras said, and took a step toward Carlotta.

The movement brought him into the light of other torches. Leprosini whimpered and Carlotta caught her breath in fear and admiration. How beautiful was death! The man was seven feet tall in his dreadlocks, with enormous shoulders and a waist slim as a girl's. His jeans were tight over his slim hips, and he trod softly in trainers like the ultimate advertisement.

"Pussy," he repeated, as if it were the only word in the world.

Alonso said, "You has no time for dat now."

"Mind your own business, Alonso," Carlotta said firmly. "What is your name, sir?"

"Don't business wid my name," Ras muttered, and put out a long hand to take hold of the shirt so recently put on, and rip it away from her. The cloth was new, and the violence of the movement took her off her feet, turned her round and threw her on the bed, from which she sprang up, her back against the wall, her arms crossed to protect her breasts.

Ras stepped closer.

"Your name does matter," Carlotta whispered, and then, recovering her calm authority, continued, "Your name does matter, because in other circumstances I'm sure we would be friends. Whatever your name is, you're behaving very badly, do you see, barging into a bedroom in the middle of the night, and you must not do what you're thinking of doing because you'd be very sorry, very sorry indeed ..."

Ras was riveted in disbelief, and even with respect, and Carlotta thought, if I can keep talking until the end of the world this thing won't happen ... I can tame the lion.

Then from outside came the sound of an outboard motor starting up and roaring away. Everyone paused to listen.

Alonso said, "No time for romance, Ras, somebody get away. You hear. Somebody gone in a motorboat. Only time to take hostage and leave."

"Maybe later," Carlotta said.

"Now," said the tall man softly.

"You'll have to get rid of them," Carlotta said decisively, and waved at the circle of torchbearers, who were crowded into the room like a parody of the Ku Klux Klan.

"Out, all of you, out! And you, Alonso!"

15

On the boat, sweating with anxiety, Stephen had the radio on, desperately seeking help. He found a Spanish voice somewhere in Santo Domingo who seemed to be drinking heavily, and then a man in Black River who said "Try Kingston," and then to his joy and surprise the voice of Romeo Foster in Bluefields, who identified himself as Jamaica Coastguard.

"This is the yacht *Swingtime.*"

Romeo, who sounded sleepy, took ages to reply. "Yes, man, yes ... I remember you, you had the Minister on board. What happen? You on a reef?"

Stephen tried his best to explain, slowly and carefully, that the yacht was all right – in fact, it was safely anchored – but the Hotel Casuarina had been invaded by bandits, the telephone line had been cut, everyone held prisoner, that he was fearful of a massacre, and would soon up anchor and get out before they came after him.

There was an even longer pause before Romeo said, "What you smokin', man?"

Stephen protested and told the whole story again, which made Romeo a little annoyed. It was bad enough to be woken by a lunatic ...

"It'll be your arse," Stephen said, "if all those tourists are murdered because you did nothing!"

"Yes, murder them, why not! You people come down to my country and think you can order me about! I know what you're doing here, and I should arrest you long ago but for the Minister."

Stephen's voice went all humble, "Please, sir, I beg you. Will you try and get through to the police, to the army or anybody!"

"You're a practical joker," Romeo said.

"Give me one more chance," Stephen pleaded. "Try to phone the Casuarina. If you can't get through will you notify the police?"

"Not getting through on the phone is not a police matter."

"It's a matter of bloody life or death!"

"Over and out," Romeo said.

The coastguardsman, in his pyjamas, his feet in sandals to keep them off the cold floor, considered the problem. It would take ten minutes to walk down to Rudolph's place, ten minutes to wake him up, and longer than that to try to telephone. He was in Bluefields, with no way to get to Negril. The bandits, if there were bandits, would have killed everybody by then and taken their possessions. Still, if he could get through to HQ he would at least have reported the rumour and he would be in the clear, which was the main thing.

***

Mass George, crawling on his stomach with an electric torch in his hand, got to the laundry room where the switchboard was and, seeing what Alonso had done, restored electricity to the hotel. In the glow of burglar lights and bedside lights, the square of buildings came alive again. The lights dispelled terror, and by making the situation clearer, made it seem much better. The Army of Jah were flushing the guests out of their bedrooms, herding them through the oleanders and assembling them in the dining room. There they all sat with hands on the tables, within a circle of automatic rifles; sat and waited.

Bonanza, in a dressing gown and horn-rimmed spectacles, and Miss Pearl, ample-bosomed and without her wig, were at the central table. Fearing that any move to violence, any exemplary execution to terrify the others, would certainly involve him, Bonanza sat quiet as a mouse, trusting to the immunity of being ordinary. Miss Pearl was more decisive by nature and kept hissing at him, "Do something. Make a proposition."

"What?"

"Buy them off."

"With what?"

"Money."

"Just be quiet, Pearl. We have no money."

"Yes, you have."

"Be quiet. It's not safe to mention it."

Bullfrog and Fonseca, on Alonso's orders, were made to stand face to the wall, with arms pressed against it, like captured gangsters.

Leprosini was under personal guard. The man holding the noose around his neck never took his eyes off him and never relaxed his grip.

"Are you going to kill me?" Leprosini said. "I've got a million dollars …"

"You got a rope aroun' your neck, dat's what you got, boy," the black man said. "Million dollars can't save you."

"What are you going to do?" Leprosini whispered.

"Stuff you wid thyme an onion an' roast you like a pig!"

***

Alonso, by the pool, was looking up at Carlotta's window. When the lights came on there had been no response from number 97. Whatever was going on in there was the same in darkness, lamplight, or in daylight too. How long, oh Lord, how long? When would the man be sated, or the woman for that matter? How much longer would that gang of cut-throats be content to sit looking at white people made ugly by the lack of make-up, clothes and hair dos – a raggle-taggle lot, like victims of a shipwreck, but still the proud possessors of rings, necklaces, wallets, passports and credit cards.

It began to rain. Sudden and violent, the water poured down into the patio, flooded the gutters, splashed into the pool and drenched the zinnias, drowned out the moaning from the dining room and soaked Alonso from head to foot. Under cover of the downpour he moved closer to Carlotta's window and stood under her balcony, water streaming down his face.

"Ras," he called. "Ras!"

There was no reply, and the noise of the rain covered whatever other noise there might have been in the water-shrouded bridal chamber.

Alonso, seized by a fit of determination, climbed the concrete steps and rapped firmly on the door. "Ras," he said, "come out! People waitin' on you, man. The army is without orders."

Silence.

"Ras!"

The reports of the automatic rifle, the splintering of the door above his head and Alonso's own cry of terror all came in an instant, and Alonso was down the stairway like a spider down a drain. Picking himself up, realising he was unhurt, he put a finger in his ear to shake the water out. A freedom fighter was running towards him. "What 'appen? What 'appen?"

"Nuttin', nuttin' no 'appen. De man still busy."

The sound of the shots had made the captives even more docile, and the unrelenting rain increased their isolation from the world. The Army of Jah, content to be in power and growing every minute in admiration of their leader, dozed over their guns.

Alonso stole away to look for Precious.

***

He tapped on her door, using the pattern of taps she would remember, and waited outside, sheltering under the overhang.

"Door open," said a soft voice, and he went in.

The room was empty.

"Precious?"

"Under de bed."

"Come out. Nobody goin' hurt you."

"I not comin' out. Somebody goin' dead."

"Nobody goin' dead."

"Den what is all dis rumpus?" said the voice under the bed. "Chrissmus?"

Her face appeared, looking up at him from the floor. "Dis is your fault, Alonso. I know you. Dis is all some jinnalship, some mischief-making, some trouble cause by you."

"Well, it gone wrong," Alonso said wearily, sitting on the bed.

Precious kept her body hidden but left her head out, to see and be seen. "What gone wrong?"

"The plan."

"What plan?"

"I tell Ras to come an' capture Leprosini. I tell him that Bonanza is here too. I tell him he can take the Yankee man to Mountain Valley an' keep him hostage an' be famous all over de world. Den he can make de CIA pay ransom, millions of *you-ess*, an' he can make Leprosini swear an' sign a paper to say Alonso is innocent! I never kill Chin Lee or anybody else! Is Bullfrog and Fonseca do it under orders. Make him sign and swear de paper, an' get me my pardon, an' my job back."

Precious was impressed. She had not thought him capable of such massive mischief. Her head came further out, like a tortoise relaxing. "So what happen?"

"Carlotta is detainin' him."

"Detainin' who?"

"Ras."

"No."

"Yes."

"Detainin' him?"

"In 97. Now."

"Englishwoman bad, eh!" cried Precious, deeply shocked. "Wicked!"

"Maybe she t'ink she makin' sacrifice," Alonso said hopefully.

"No." Precious was quite definite. "Woman don't sacrifice. A woman is sacrifice a'ready."

Alonso did not think the remark was worth an answer. It was pure nonsense, but he would humour her by pretending to agree. "Life is hard," he said, and then returned to his own problems. "Trouble is, Ras don't see a woman for months, years, maybe never. How long, oh Lord, how long!"

***

The police car arrived at the crack of dawn. The blue light was flashing self-importantly and there was no need for the siren, Swaby thought. He and three constables could sort this one out, get to the bottom of the rumour, and radio to Kingston, 'All is well'.

The firing started as soon as the car swung between the concrete posts marked 'IN' and continued as the car slowed by the front entrance. Only when a constable in the back seat squealed in pain and the windscreen in front of him shattered did Swaby realise that someone was firing at him. The driver tumbled to it at the same time, threw the car into second, stood on the accelerator, and disappeared in a shower of gravel between the posts marked 'OUT'.

The situation was getting serious, but there was no way Alonso was going to knock on the door of number 97 again.

The man was not deaf, and if he didn't want to know what the shooting was about, there was no point in telling him. It was going to get worse before it got better, he said to Precious; it was going to be a bad day, perhaps even his last. The only remedy was breakfast. With Precious in tow, he located Madame Juliette and persuaded her to open the kitchen and get the girls working on johnny-cakes, coffee, hard dough, saltfish and callaloo, anything that was to hand.

Alonso moved on to the dining room and confronted the survivors of the Titanic and their sleepy guards. "Breafus' cookin'!" he announced.

The Army of Jah perked up sharpish, but the tourists, among them Leprosini, Bonanza, and their friends facing the wall, just groaned, or stared back in disbelief.

"Knives is not allowed," Alonso said, "forks neither, so you will have to eat wid your fingers or dip de bread. So jus' settle back an' relax; food coming."

A woman from South Carolina asked if her children could have some water.

"Why didn' ask before?" Alonso said. "This is the Army of Jah, you know. We are not savages. Precious, you can circulate a pitcher and a mug."

So began breakfast at the Casuarina, not unlike the feeding of the five thousand, for those who feared death took small bites and were generous to their neighbours, hoping for eternal life.

***

Swaby had not been idle. He had set up road blocks a few hundred yards away in both directions. Early morning traffic pulling up behind was made to park sideways across the lanes and drivers to hand their ignition keys to the police.

He set snipers on the beach, hidden in the undergrowth. The bastards who had fired on him would have to come on foot; they could not leave by road or go to sea except as targets.

His radio hot with supplication, he waited for reinforcement.

***

Precious was pouring coffee when Ras appeared, cool, neat and walking slowly. The Army rested their rifles and cheered, a chorus of envious congratulation, a loud affectionate salute to the power of the life force.

"You want coffee?" Alonso asked.

"We has no time to spare," Ras trumpeted. "Bring de truck, load up de hostage dem an' leave!"

"Easier said than done," Alonso said. "By now de hotel is surrounded, an' we mus' fight our way out."

"No problem," Ras replied confidently. "We just tie de American and de Minister on the bonnet, an' tourists all around de side. Nobody will shoot at us."

He sent a volunteer to get the truck which had been hidden in the vacant lot next door. A solitary rifle shot was all that was ever heard of him again.

Just then the helicopter came, a large black flying crab, down the length of the beach, swooping, circling, its chattering engine threatening, passed over the hotel, having a look. Bold freedom fighters took pot shots at it, wasting ammunition.

"Das not police, dat is Jamaica Defence Force. We has de army to contend wid now! What to do?"

Ras blinked and scowled; he looked like thunder but was too weak to think. The lion of Judah was a spent pussycat. Alonso must be General.

"We walk around an' check de position of our fire power, an' den consult as to de next move."

"Right," said Ras.

They did that. Every approach to the hotel was covered. They persuaded Mass George to open the bar, and with a bottle of rum between them sat down to think. They were constantly interrupted by requests from the hostages to go to the bathroom, which were all allowed except for the Minister and Leprosini.

"Let them stew in deir own juice," was Ras's uncharitable response.

"As we have all dese hostages, de police can not attack us," he said to Alonso.

"We can't get away neither," Alonso concluded.

"Might as well take it easy," Ras said with a wistful glance toward number 97.

"You couldn't climb de steps," Alonso said.

These reflections were interrupted by a loudhailer, which seemed to be mounted on a van out on the main road. "You in there! Whoever you are, come out! Come out now! You are surrounded by superior force! Come out with your hands up!"

Ras took a swallow of rum, which seemed to raise his fighting spirits. "Tell dem we goin' to kill de children first, one by one."

This message was passed from the dining room, across the patio, echoed by the voices of the Army of Jah, and bawled *fortissimo* from the window over reception, where a freedom fighter crouched under a potted palm. "We goin' kill de children firs'!"

Alonso was worried. "I don't think you should say t'ings like dat, Ras. T'ings will go from bad to worse, and nothin' gained."

"What you want me to do? Surrender?"

"No. I want to talk. Bring Bonanza here, and Mr Leprosy."

"Right," said Ras.

189

The two men were allowed to go to the bathroom, returned, and sat down with a rum in hand.

"I only drink Perrier," Leprosini said. "It's healthier."

"Drink de rum!" Ras ordered and turned to his lieutenant. "What you want to talk about, Alonso?"

Before Alonso could devise his terms, there was a shout from the reception sentry, "White flag comin'!"

"Ready to shoot!" Ras said.

Through reception into the patio garden came Swaby, the fat inspector, and a young man in the uniform of the Jamaica Defence Force, armed with a moustache and a swagger stick.

"Dat's better," Ras said. "Bring dem in here an' we can settle de whole business."

A conference table was arranged and Madame Juliette decorated it with fresh flowers and three bottles of Appleton Gold, asking at the same time that they should settle their differences before lunch as she had a hotel to run.

"I want a million *you-ess*," Ras began, a man of few words.

Leprosini felt at home at last. This was his territory. "You must be crazy. Who's got that kind of money?"

"You do," Bonanza said. "You have a suitcase full."

"What are you talking about, Magnus? That's just holiday cash."

Bonanza, who had been cheated and spent a miserable night, would not let go. "It's a hell of a lot more than that."

"Where is de money?" Ras wanted to know.

"Under the bed you were sleeping in."

Ras put his head back and cackled like a chicken. "All dat money, and make up to de million, and I want safe passage for de Army of Jah."

"How far?"

"Until we gone, up de mountain."

"And you will let all these people go?" said the officer with the moustache.

"Maybe," Ras said, pouring himself another rum. "Understand, the Yankee man comin' wid me. Safe passage is not safe widout him. Unless I keep him, you will unleash helicopter, soldier, all dose t'ings on me. I keep de Yankee man until de whole million come. One likkle suitcase not enough. I want money by bag and bushel, special delivery from CIA, and I am in my forest where I hide till I arise and conquer!"

"Sure, sure, all that can be arranged," said Leprosini. "We can make a deal."

"Not so fast!" Alonso said. "My terms! I want a paper say is not me kill Chin Lee, because it is not me, and dat is de cause of all dis botheration."

Swaby looked at Bonanza. "I don't think we can drop the murder charge, do you, Minister, without evidence, or a case against somebody else?"

"Unless my little frien' go free," Ras said, "I kill de children one by one, an' torture de Yankee man until he beg to die."

"It's possible you made a mistake, Inspector," Bonanza said, and Leprosini, remembering he had not paid Fonseca and Bullfrog, and remembering also that he would need all the cash he could get, said, "Yeah, it's real possible."

Through the doorway to the dining room, Leprosini could see the man in the blue suit, a lonely hostage. Unlike the other guests, a man on business. Leprosini caught his eye and nodded, and the man turned toward the alligator and the squashed man with their hands pressed against the wall, awaiting execution.

"Then that's agreed," Bonanza said. "Alonso, the charges are dropped. Consider yourself not guilty."

16

The sea being calm and the wind behind, Carlotta sat before the mast, leaning on the cabin roof. She wore a loose white cotton shirt and shorts. Her incomparable legs were bare, drawn up, embraced, so she would rest her cheek on her knees, or looking up, see beyond the bow to the blue expanse of ocean with no shore, no distant islands and no home.

So that was that. The ultimate bonk. What a tenuous connection there was between the present and the past, between memory and reality. She had a bruise on the inside of her left thigh, one on the shoulder and probably others that she could not see. The bruising wouldn't last and the night itself would fade and be forgotten, only to return fresh and complete, tasted and endured, in times of loneliness or unfulfilled desire.

She had wanted to give everything, and had, but in the conflict of love-making had she also sought humiliation? After coitus all animals are sad and she had a special capacity for sadness. But she was not humiliated; stretching her legs she could still feel the wondrous sensuality, the relaxation, the glow of all her senses. He was magnificent and yet, when it was over it was he, collapsed and soft, who lay, his great body in her arms, all unprotected. She could have cut the dreadlocks off and called the men to blind him.

She had not wanted humiliation or conquest, but to find herself complete, and that had happened, but it was past, and only made her incompleteness plain. What could she do now? Settling down in Mountain Valley was quite out of the question and the thought of enduring his male arrogance in daily circumstances was quite intolerable. Having him in tow, a gelded giant at her beck and call, would be the worst possible of outcomes.

What could she do? She'd had the best of it, which could only be repeated and which, if the truth be told, she did not want again. Beyond the bow of the boat, the horizon was harsh and hot, the ocean dark and cold. It was terribly inviting. But there was nothing under the water and something over the horizon, pleasant or unpleasant hardly mattered. Carlotta, accustomed to despair, was not quite ready for The End. If 'I want', 'I promise' or 'I love' turn to dust, there is always simple comfort to be had in 'To be continued'.

***

Leprosini enjoyed his sojourn in Mountain Valley. He loved the pure fresh air, sleeping under the stars and resting in the shade; he loved the movement of the clouds over the green mountains and the patches of ethereal blue above. The black fellows treated him well, laughing at his ineptitudes, caring for him as if he were a cripple or a child learning to walk. He drank water from a spring, learned which fruit to eat and which to leave, how to catch shrimp in a basket and how to hang, kill, butcher and roast a wild hog.

He was saddened when the helicopters came, great bulky things with blades at either end, settling like missionaries by the Baptist Church, bringing baskets of money and boxes full of death, the unused leftovers of his country's wars. They brought him freedom, and brought wealth and power to Ras Clawt and the Army of Jah. Leprosini flew home to a hero's welcome. Please no ticker tape.

Two weeks later, at the request of the Jamaican government, of course, a flight of F-111s from Guantanamo destroyed Mountain Valley. The whole hillside was a black scar visible from satellites. Miss Kelly's grocery store made up its mind and slid down to the valley floor. The Baptist Church had neither roof nor walls. Ammunition had exploded and guns were tossed like matchsticks every way. Thatch cottages were little piles of windblown ash. The ganja fields were gone. Local inhabitants were burned, and twisted bodies hung on defoliated branches like runaway slaves in iron cages. Even the forest birds were silent, and the dry black earth waited empty for the mercy of the rain.

But Ras and the Army of Jah were not there. On Leprosini's departure, Ras had ordered a retreat and taken refuge in the Cockpit Country, on the dark green floor of a crater, waiting for the fury of power to pass, for as Alonso said, "Him dat fight an' run away, live to fight anoddah day."

***

The charges against Alonso had indeed been dropped and the bullet-riddled bodies of Fonseca and Bullfrog had been recovered from the white Toyota van, found by a fisherman lying on its side half-submerged in the shallow waters off Prickle Point. Any involvement with Bonanza or Leprosini was too tenuous for investigation, the stuff of gossip not law.

Alonso got his job back – not so much a job as a comfortable berth. There were three square five-star meals a day, taken in the shade behind the kitchen, long walks along the beach and through the gardens, checking on locks and doors and lights on cars, and sleeping in the arms of Precious Ting, who in a moment of weakness had promised to make a baby for him.

It was a surprise when Mass George called him into the office, with Madame Juliette at her desk, back turned, pretending not to listen. "Sorry, Alonso, but you have to go."

"Go?"

"Yes, you're fired."

"But I'm not hired yet, Mass George. I does but eat and sleep."

"That's the problem. We can't afford to feed you any longer. You eat too much."

Alonso's universe was sucked into a black hole. "Eat too much," he repeated blankly.

"Tell me, Alonso. When you are doing the rounds of the hotel, you notice anything in particular?"

"No, sir. If I notice anything, I does report it."

"You don't notice that we have no guests?"

"No guests?"

"Since the troubles, Alonso – you know what I mean – we have a shortage of tourists. Travel agents all across America just put a line through the Casuarina Hotel. We come second after Baghdad but ahead of Kabul and North Korea as a place for American tourists not to go. The Casuarina Hotel, Negril, Jamaica, is the place where guerrillas, led by the night watchman, took over the hotel, and robbed, raped and murdered men, women and children all alike. We're going broke, Alonso! We're in a Third World country with a currency crisis and a revolution coming. We're a lost cause! You take my meaning? You, Alonso, are to blame, and you are expendable! Go!"

"I am to blame for all dat?"

"Yes, Alonso, go! Get your backside off my property!"

"Wait a minute, Mass George. Cease de bad language, listen and gimme a chance! I has a plan. You and me can fix up dis whole business, organise a happy ending. You just has to advertise, to propaganda, to noise abroad that all is well, that drugs and war finish on de island, dat dere is nuttin' leave but peace and love. Peace and love! Say dat, and they will all return to Jamaica!"

The End